THE LAND'S HERITAGE

BOOK THREE

THE NEW LIFE SERIES

BY

LOUISE BOUCK

ACKNOWLEDGEMENTS

It is important to say thank you to all the people who continue to encourage me. I give a special thank you to Mary Koestner. Thank you, dear friend, for your prayer support. A big thank you goes to my husband, Dale Bouck, who managed to keep my computer running in spite of the monsoons and act as my editor as well. A big thank you hug to R.J. Dick who was the first to want to read "The Story of Ben Slater" and to Brenda Dick who read "The Story of Sarah" to RJ when he was ill, and thanks to Donna Shaw, who enthusiastically helped me to keep Sarah's feet on the right path.

Thank you to Ray Shaw, who helped me, very patiently, to gain confidence with technology that I needed to learn. Without his expert help this series would still be a set of files in my computer.

Thank you to the staff at the computer lab for their technical help. What would any of us do without the public libraries and the wonderful people that work there?

The New Life Series   Book 3   by Louise Bouck

Permissions

Copyright

Registration Number TXu 1-894-9722

Register of Copyrights, United States of America

December 12, 2013

Copyright Claimant Louise Irene Bouck

This book is a work of fiction. Any resemblance to actual events or persons living or dead is entirely coincidental.

ISBN 13 978 1-943984-12-1 E-book

ISBN 13 978-1-943984-02-2 Paperback

Hisgivenstories LIB Publications

DEDICATION

This New Life Series is dedicated to Jesus, and to my family, those that have gone before me, those who are with me and those to come, and all my brothers and sisters in Christ.

✝

The New Life Series   Book 3   by Louise Bouck

TABLE OF CONTENTS

INTRODUCTION

This is book three in "The New Life Series." The Christian fiction in this series is written to offer the reader a wholesome entertainment, starting back in a simpler but not easier time. The example of spiritual strength and "never quit" attitude is refreshing and inspiring. The adventurers follow the trail to a new land and challenges they never imagined.

In book one *"More Than Survival,"* follow Benjamin Slater as he copes with the wild isolation of the new frontier and the lessons of self-preservation as he experiences the pain of loss and joys of accomplishment. He travels *"Life's Many Journeys,"* book two and learns to appreciate *"The Land's Heritage,"* in Book three, as the people of the settlement show their gratitude. In Book four, you will find out *"The Story of Sarah."*

As you read the books, Ben develops into a man of physical and spiritual strength. His problem solving mind is challenged many times.

When Sarah, his sister returns to him and they are *"Together,"* book five. You will find out how her life affected the Indians that took her and how they became *"The Blue Stone People,"* in book six.

A change of scene takes you to the camp of the Sentu and three survivors enter the story, in book seven *"Teewahpanee the Boy, Two Feathers the Man,"* Willow and Water Bug. Together they bring new strength and young blood to an old people. With Willow at his side in book eight he becomes leader of *"The People of The Lion."* He is chosen by the Lion of Judah to be a rescuer, and is rewarded in book nine, by being allowed to discover *"The Lion's Den."*

In book ten the land that Ben Slater's father chose has miraculously remained with the family as time has gone by and generations were born.

In a day beyond today the series skips to the final times after the rapture. A new heroine stands up bravely to the soldiers of the anti-Christ. She finds Ben's Bible, Mary Slater's journal and the gift of faith. Emily spreads the word struggling to survive the time of tribulation as she finally realizes that this is *"Just the Beginning"* for those who believe.

CHAPTER ONE   WAGONS AND PEOPLE

One evening in spring, Beth carried Johnny to the barn to tell the men that the meal was ready but she could not find them. The horses were out. All was quiet, and then she spotted both of them gazing into the distance down river from the top of the bluff. Her heart missed a beat as a stone of fear settled into her chest. She was questioning them before they were far enough down to hear what she was saying.

"What did you see? What were you looking at? Are the Indians coming back?"

"No it isn't Indians. It is too far away to see what it is but it isn't Indians."

"It looks like wagons and riders and they are headed up river, close to the trees on the other side!

"I'm excited!" squealed Beth. "Let's go meet them and talk to them. I wish I had baked today, but we can offer them something to eat and maybe they can come to camp and stay the night and…"

"Stop," said Ben. "We have no idea who they are or what kind of people they are. It might be better to stay out of sight and see if we can find out more about them before we start thinking about entertaining anyone."

"Ben is right," said Jed, her husband. "Let's just be cautious."

It was apparent that Beth was eager for company. She probably wants to talk with other women about the

9

baby, thought Jed. Maybe I could go to the settlement and ask Rose to come visit for a few days. But it would be better if she came after our cabin is built. Her house is nice. I don't know how she would feel about no privacy and dirt floors. He wanted Beth to be happy. He would give it more thought.

"Honey, is the meal ready?" he asked to distract her.

"Yes, that is why I came out to find you. I hope the vegetables aren't burned," she muttered as she hurried inside to check them. Both men ate their food so fast that she was sure they didn't taste a thing. Sometimes they are like children, she thought. They can't wait to get back up there to see how close the wagons are. I wonder if it is people looking for a place to homestead. I hope they choose a place near here so that we can visit.

She fed the baby and changed his diaper and rocked him to sleep. She closed the window after making him cozy in his beautiful handmade cradle. She ran her hand over the moon and stars on the headboard, appreciating the craftsmanship of Jed and Ben.

She had noticed the cool of the late afternoon air and pulled the curtain shut on the bedroom doorway before going outside to find out if they could tell who or what was traveling on the prairie. Jed and Ben came hurrying back down. Jed hugging Beth announced that it looked like the entire settlement was coming!

"Oh Jed, maybe the Indians burned them out!" Tears filled her eyes.

"I'll go get Johnny, and then let's go meet them."

Just before leaving the hut, she put their biggest pan filled with water on to heat. She quickly crumbled in handfuls of mint and one of lemon grass. There she thought, at least we will have tea to offer them. She hurried out the door with Johnny in her arms.

She had wrapped him in the blanket she had made from the unborn buffalo calf hide. Her dark brown leather dress was fringed at the bottom and her shoes were handmade moccasins, dyed in the same dark brown. She had decorated the long sleeves of her dress with beads made by cutting through bone and sanding them smooth. Jed had helped to make them. She had pulled her beautiful dark brown hair back and caught it in a matching piece of leather. She looked down at her dress. I wish that I had chosen the little cotton dress that I made. I look like an Indian with these clothes on. I hope they haven't had trouble with the Indians, she thought, as she slipped into her black wolf fur coat and hurried to the river.

Jed held the baby while she got on Ginger. The river was low and Ginger crossed without having to swim. All she got wet was her legs and the bottom of her stomach. Ben had put a padded hide across Ginger's back with a braided strap that secured it, for Beth to sit on. She created the perfect image of the Indian Madonna and child as she cradled her small baby boy. Ginger was so gentle and steady she seemed to understand the preciousness of the load on her back. She kept up with

Ben and Jed, walking between them with no lead attached.

The people of the settlement moved slowly along. Some rode but many walked. They were puzzled that they had not found Jed and Ben's camp by now.

*****

"It can't be this far. We must have missed it. Maybe it is on the other side of the river. If we don't spot it soon, we should turn back," said Tom.

Henry, Sam and Helen's oldest son, ran back and forth teasing two little girls, the daughters of the new blacksmith, Matthew Morgan and Lizzy his wife. His shop was just across the street from Sam and Helen's General Store and Trading Post. Gentle Fawn, Tom's wife and their little twins rode along in a wagon filled with boxes, barrels and bundles each one wrapped and padded so well that its contents were indiscernible.

A chuck wagon followed along that had been used to make communal meals since the beginning of their trip five days earlier.

A third, fourth and fifth big wagon, pulled by strong teams, followed, two stacked with lumber and the third had a load of wood shingles on top of a layer of heavy beams. Somewhere in the loads precious windows rode, well-padded and protected. The caravan had taken the route up the Silver River and crossed where the wagon trains had, then followed the trail for a short distance, cutting back at an angle to the Hickory.

A loud cheer went up from the travelers as they spotted the little group approaching them.

As soon as Beth was lifted down she ran to hug Helen and Rose. Tom helped Gentle Fawn from the wagon and she joined in the group hug. Everyone was laughing and talking at once.

It would be dark soon.

Beth remembered her big kettle of tea and told the ladies to come with her to the hut. Ben helped ferry them across.

Other women began to set up tents and a large fire was started in a clearing away from the trees. The chuck wagon pulled up and the man that rode on it started to get out huge kettles. Sam and Tom still had not told Jed why they were here. They were waiting until everyone was together gathered around the fire.

Beth felt silly now bringing her friends across the river for a cup of tea. They probably had plenty in that chuck wagon, she thought, as she carefully picked her way up the branch and rock path to the hut.

Once inside, the ladies hugged again and told her that they loved the place. The furniture was comfortable. Beth had made pads for the chairs. She had sanded the benches and oiled them until they were satin smooth. She poured the tea and set the honey container on the table with a bowl holding several spoons. They enjoyed their tea and chatted and laughed but didn't spoil the surprise.

"Let's take your bed rolls over on the raft so that you can spend the night over there with us," suggested Helen.

"That's what I was thinking, too," said Rose. They helped her gather what she would need for the baby and then, with their arms full, they picked their way back to the water carefully using the rocks and branches, following her example.

Beth led the way with the baby on one arm and the lantern held high so the others could see. The moon was not full, but bright enough to add some light. Ben had gone back with a lantern from the barn and Tom had the raft ready to transport the ladies to the big fire and waiting celebration meal.

As soon as Beth stepped through the trees where she could be seen, another big cheer went up. She felt embarrassed, but filled with pleasure at the warmth of their friendship. A deer roasted over the fire, while pots of wonderful smelling concoctions simmered on the side. Coffee pots filled the air with added aroma.

After everyone was settled on blankets or hides near the fire; Tom stood up and offered a prayer of thanks that they had arrived safely and found their friends well and happy. He prayed a blessing on the food and everyone started talking and eating.

Beth had wanted company, but she couldn't believe her eyes as she looked around. An entire settlement had traveled five days, just to come here to be with them. She met three new families that had also come along. It felt wonderful, but a little sad, too. She wished that she lived closer so she could see these people more often.

Jed stood up and proudly and quite formally introduced Jonathon Benjamin Jones. He held him up in the fire light for everyone to see. They applauded and woke him and he let out a wail that made everyone laugh.

"He may be little, but he is loud!" said Jed. And everyone laughed again.

Tom stood up again. This time he had a serious look on his face.

"Jed, we all came here because we wanted to thank you properly for coming to warn us about the Indian war party. You took a chance on getting killed yourself. You could have stayed hidden and they would not have known you were here, but you didn't. You struggled against the freezing river and took a canoe down life threatening rapids to save all our lives. We all appreciate your friendship and strength of character and we are all here to thank you for warning us. Because we had time to prepare, we didn't lose one person. Not one building in the settlement was burned. The Steven's house at the crossing was burned but they were safe because of your warning. We owe you our lives. We have come to build your house and won't leave until it is completed. We have lumber from Tom's sawmill, and nails and three windows!"

Another loud cheer went up and Gentle Fawn's twin babies started crying.

Stump barked and shook water all over Ben. Bold One had followed but she was overwhelmed by the number of people and had hidden in the bushes.

Jed stood up. His face was red and his hands shook a little. He was unable to say what he was feeling.

"Thank You," he said quickly and sat back down.

"No, we are trying to thank you," said Sam laughing.

Ben stood up and got everyone's attention.

"This is Stump," he said. "He has a wolf wife named Bold One and two beautiful pups. So if you see a gray and white wolf hanging around, don't shoot her. She is friendly and has saved us from an attack by a mountain lion. She actually guards our camp just as Stump does."

A murmur went through the camp. Some were voicing amazement while others concern for their children.

"Please understand. Bold One spent the winter with us in the barn with our horses and some chickens. She is no ordinary wolf," said Ben. More murmurs and exclamations could be heard.

"Don't worry, Ben, we didn't come here to kill anything. So long as she stays her distance, no one will hurt her," said Tom. "After all it must be safe if Beth's baby is near it and she isn't concerned."

Beth got acquainted with the new women and was pleased that they had all decided to come and help.

16

Everyone talked until it was very late. The man that brought the chuck wagon, produced wonderful apple cakes, and then politely announced that they were to accompany, the last big pot of coffee he was making until morning. He had set up a tent near his wagon and at that point he went in the tent and got in his bedroll. Most of the folks were tired from their days of traveling and took that as their signal to settle into quieter conversations, from their bedrolls. Finally the many people were quiet. The big fire was banked and only Ben, Jed and Beth were still too excited to sleep.

The camp was buzzing at daybreak. A very large raft was created to ferry supplies from the wagons across the river. Long before noon, horses were busy dragging skids of lumber to the cabin site. The women cooked and watched the proceedings as each trip brought more supplies.

Several walked around on the hill and nodded to each other their approval of the location. The next thing they did was to tell Sam and Tom that the rooms had to be larger!

"Is that the only opinion women have when a house is being built?" asked one of the men, as they all moaned and laughed.

Several voiced concerns over the isolation of the homestead. They thought Jed's idea to put a hidden room under the storage shed was a very good one and when Ben volunteered to start digging it, others joined in.

As soon as the dimensions were established, the hole began to appear. The loose dirt was piled on the empty skids, as the lumber was removed, the horses returned to the river crossing, with dirt for the new addition on the hut. The men talked to Ben about the horses and his hut and Ben told them how they caught the horses and how the hut came to look more like a mound or hill than a cabin.

As the day continued, and the piles of supplies and stacks of lumber appeared near the cabin site, several men said they had climbed the bluff to see the boulder that had smashed into the roof of the hut. They thought Ben's idea of moving the main room forward was a good one.

"I did think you should put a roof over the boulder area so it cannot be seen from above. It will make a good space to hide in or an escape route," said Paul Carter, one of the new residents in the settlement.

"You are right," said Ben. "I just haven't really had time to do it. We have been pretty busy."

"It couldn't have been very easy living in the barn in the winter," said one of the men.

"Actually we were lucky to have it finished so we could use it. The wolf and pups soon learned their area. I was a little worried when we had to take the chicks in there with the wolves so near, but she seemed to understand that they were special. She never bothered them at all. We were warm enough, and had plenty of food. I had the new roof of the hut done just before Christmas," he said.

"It was difficult when Jed burned his hand. I'm not much of a nurse, and Beth turned her ankle bad, that same night. Some days the snow was pretty deep and we kept the horses in. Oh well, it all worked out."

"It is amazing what you have here," said one of the men. They chatted about this and that as the work continued. The air was scented by the newly cut lumber and freshly dug earth. Ben thought he would remember the sweet mingled scents for the rest of his life.

"That's quite a story about the way you trapped the horses in the river. It's a good idea. They can't go as fast in the water. They're less apt to get away from you that way. That white colored guy is a beauty. I wouldn't mind buying him. I wonder what Jed would take for him."

The man speaking had not been introduced to Ben. He appeared middle aged and weathered by the sun, wind and time. Ben held out his hand and said his name was Ben.

The stranger replied.

"Gray, John Gray."

"Nice to meet you," said Ben

"The horse's name is Buddy. He is mine. He's not for sale."

"Sorry, someone told me that this place belongs to Jed," the man said sarcastically and walked away. He seems to have a chip on his shoulder, thought Ben.

"Hey Ben, are we going to try to put that tunnel in now, too?" asked one of the men leaning on a shovel handle. He had heard the comment by Gray and was trying to avert a problem.

"I don't know, I guess it should be done now. It would be easier than trying to do it after the building is over this end," answered Ben. Matthew Morgan, the settlement's new blacksmith, jumped down into the hole and took a shovel from Ben.

"Let me boost you up so you can get a drink and rest. I will take over for a while. You said Jed wants a tunnel? Where's it going?"

"Not far, maybe twenty feet into the woods, just in case they would need to slip out."

"Sounds like a good idea to me, I'll get started. The only problem with this place is that it is visible from the top of the bluff. It is isolated too. It would be easy to raid. The tunnel will give Jed a little peace of mind. I used to work in a coal mine so it won't bother me none. I'll try to head it over there to come up behind that bunch of pines. We may have trouble with a lot of tree roots but it can be done."

"That's great Matthew," said Ben. He gave Ben a leg up and took over the shovel that Ben had been using. Ben handed a water bag down to the other man in the hole, and then went to look for Jed. The last load of timber was being brought down the path by the lake and Jed was with it. Jed hugged Ben and slapped his back grinning with joy.

"Hey, where have you been? I have been looking for you," said Jed. "Beth and some of the women want to know if it is all right if they start working on the garden. They are over there."

Ben went in that direction to find two men just finishing sanding new handles on the burned plow. They had sanded the blade and sharpened it. One had adapted the harness from the skid his horse had been pulling.

"That should do it," he said just as Ben walked up.

"That's a great job. Thanks. Hi, I'm Ben."

"Hello, I'm Calvin Briggs. Minnie and me, we moved here from a farm in Kansas. We jist arrived the day before everyone headed here so we tagged along. Wanted tah git tah know folks. That's my daughter Melanie over there. She's the one with the red hair. She looks jist like her Grandmah."

Ben automatically looked in the direction the man pointed. What he saw was the most beautiful girl he had ever laid eyes on. She had a sunbonnet tied around her neck but it lay on her back where the wind had blown it. Her hair was the color of gold and copper. She was round and rosy. Someone was saying something funny because all the ladies in the group were laughing. The cotton dress she wore was pale pink, with a lime green sash, tied in a big bow in the back. Ben couldn't take his eyes off her.

"She's a fiery one. Her temper is as big as that barn!" said Calvin.

"Is it ok with you if I work up the ground? The women want to plant the garden," said Calvin.

"Oh, sure," said Ben, forcing himself to turn back to Calvin.

"Go ahead, but I think Beth wanted to make it bigger this year. Maybe I should pull out the end posts now and then I can put up what new fence is needed before the stuff sprouts," explained Ben.

"I can do that with Bessie here," said Calvin. "She loves to pull. We pulled durn near a hundred stumps one year to clear five acres on my Pa's place. He had good land by the river, but my place was dry as dust. I finally figured I had to move or starve. My brother's there on Pa's farm with his wife and five kids."

Ben shook Calvin's hand.

"It's a real pleasure to meet you Calvin. Thanks for coming along and helping," said Ben, as he headed up the path. It looked more like a country road now, after so many horses and skids had passed over it. He glanced back at the group of women. Melanie was looking his way and smiled a coy smile before quickly looking away.

When he stepped out of the trees near the hut, he discovered a group of three men with a huge pile of thick branches, working at covering the hole that the boulder had made in the roof of the hut. He greeted the men and introduced himself, shaking hands all around.

"Hope you don't mind us doing this" said one of them. "We will leave the corner section loose so that it can be pushed out in case of emergency."

"Everything is getting done at once," said Ben. "I am so excited; I can't express how grateful I am to all of you for coming and helping us."

"We are glad to do it," answered a man inside the back of the hut, standing beside the boulder. He was hooking the bottom of the branches together with heavy cord and then pegging them to secure the ceiling.

"We thought as long as so many of us are here we may as well bring a couple skids of soil and get it up over the roof for you if you want. We will thatch this part with willow and then grass first. We can see that's how the rest is." Ben was unable to speak. He had a lump in his throat. No one had ever been this kind to him.

Finally he nodded.

"Thank you, all of you," and walked back toward the trail to the lake.

Ben discovered that Bold One had taken the pups and was keeping them in the old den. She nipped and growled when she heard him coming down the trail, forcing them inside. It is just as well he thought. After everyone settles down tonight, I will bring some food and put water near the den.

Ben slipped to a quiet spot behind the clump of pine trees and on his knees he entered the presence of God. At that moment he thought that nothing could distract him from praising and worshipping God and offering thanksgiving for all the favor and blessings that he saw all around him, after a moment he felt a tug on his shirt. Rascal was doing his best to turn it into play time. Ben lifted the wiggly little pup and carried him back to the den. He realized that it was the closest he had ever been to the den. He always stopped on the grass and peeked under the pines.

When he reached the hill by the lake, the first rows of uprights were going in place. It was apparent that many of the men present had done this before. They worked as a team. They had enlarged on Jed's floor plan, but kept the same basic layout. This was going to be a wonderful house.

The ladies had coaxed Calvin into nearly doubling the garden size. They had dragged the end post down toward the woods and told him that they wanted everything in between worked up. After plowing it, he had gone to the woods with his axe to cut more posts and branches to continue the fence.

The three men had finished the roof of Ben's hut, and had chipped hand and toe holds in the part of the bluff that was inside the room with the boulder. Outside they had continued to the top, without the work being obvious from the yard near the hut. They had made an easy, quick escape route, to the top. Then they joined in the garden effort. Two had hoes and were breaking up the clumps of new sod, removing the grass and roots, tossing it out of the garden area. The third was in the woods helping Calvin. Ben decided he would join them.

He retrieved the crosscut saw from the barn and as he stepped into the trees he was handed a water jug by Melanie.

"Your face is a bit red. You look like you should take a drink of water."

"Thank you. You are very thoughtful," he said flashing his brightest smile. I could look at her the rest of my life, he thought, as he walked over to help with the wood for the fence. Together they had enough posts cut by the time the soil was readied for planting.

CHAPTER TWO   FELLOWSHIP, WORK AND A THIEF

In late afternoon the ladies took time to go up around the bend of the river just out of sight, and enjoyed a bath and fresh clothing, while the dresses they had been wearing were washed and hung over bushes to dry.

They felt like they were all on vacation. They enjoyed having other ladies to talk to and being able to help Beth was a bonus. They had become friends for life. They cuddled Johnny, and gave Beth advice. They brushed out each other's long hair and braided it, twisting the braids into large buns on the back of their heads or twisting it and securing it with pins under their sun bonnets. Melanie's hair was scooped up on top of her head with two pearl combs. She had cut it just below her shoulders and refused to braid it.

"That's so old fashioned," she told them.

When they stopped work for the day, the men took the crossing as their opportunity to get clean. They scrubbed themselves dipping under the water with their clothes on. They walked up to the campfire dripping, but felt tired and refreshed at the same time, knowing that the big campfire and warm evening breeze would soon dry their hair and clothes.

"I feel a lot better," said Slim Parker, another new pioneer, but I think some of us can't deny sore muscles," and he pointed at Sam.

"I heard you groan when you pulled that load of dirt into the woods."

"Shop keepers are in that business for a reason," said Sam laughing. "Since we finished the back of my store I haven't been working as hard. I admit it but I am enjoying every minute of this." Others agreed that they were enjoying it, too.

Most of them were not wearing leather. Jed and Ben spot cleaned their duds and washed themselves and then poled over on the small raft. That evening, everyone enjoyed crossing the river to gather at the big communal campfire and delicious meal that was waiting. During the day they had all made do with the more than ample leftovers from the feast of the night before. Children were scrubbed, fed and tucked into their beds. They were as tired as the adults from running around playing together all day. A couple of the women sat with quilt blocks on their laps, their needles busy. One of them looked up from her sewing to ask if everyone else had their blocks finished. They said they had, all but Minnie.

"I'm afraid all I have to contribute will be my stitches on the seams this time," she said.

"That's all right dear, you weren't around to even know about the quilt, in time to stitch a block," said Helen. I'm sure we will be able to make something pretty with what we have."

Calvin asked if anyone was willing to go scour the riverbank in the morning to find the right rocks for the fireplace and chimney. He acquired several volunteers.

Matthew Morgan suggested that he would like someone to go hunting with him in the morning. Ben volunteered.

"I would like to go right after I take care of the animals." Saying that reminded him of the wolf den and in a few minutes he quietly left the circle and crossed to the hut to get bear jerky. He got a big waterproof basket and filled it from the lake and placed it near the mouth of the den. Bold One saw him but did not come out. She stayed in the mouth of the den blocking the pups from coming out. She was obviously frightened by all the commotion and people. Stump on the other hand was enjoying all of it. He was getting pets and attention from everyone.

Leaving the den, Ben rounded the bend in the path near the corral gate. John Gray, the man that had mentioned Buddy earlier was leading him away from the barn.

"Hey what are you doing, John?" asked Ben.

"I thought I'd take him out and see if I like him before I make a serious offer," said the man.

"What? I told you Buddy belongs to me and he is not for sale. You have no right touching that horse!" Ben instinctively knew that had he come along a few minutes later that John and Buddy would have been gone. The man's face turned to a snarl.

"I usually get what I want, one way or another," he said, pulling a knife from his belt. He let go of the rope he had tied around Buddy's neck and started toward Ben swinging the knife back and forth in front of him. Ben was unarmed and wasn't sure what to do. With all the people around he had not been carrying his rifle.

Just then a blur of fur flashed in front of him! Bold One slammed into the man's chest with all her weight. John Gray fell hard to the ground, causing him to release the knife as he struggled with her, and then she went for his throat! He was mortally wounded.

She continued to growl loudly, showing her teeth, she stood with two front feet on his chest, and John Gray's blood on her mouth, as people came to investigate.

"My God!" said Tom. "The wolf has killed someone."

"Tom, she is protecting me. I caught this man stealing Buddy, and he pulled a knife. He was coming at me with it when she jumped him. Look, everyone, there is the knife on the ground. Let's all back up so she will calm down," said Ben. Someone in the dark of the trees cocked his gun.

"I'm not leaving an animal like that around my wife and boys! I don't care what the reason is. That wolf is a man killer!" He fired before anyone could stop him. Bold One slumped. He shot again.

The group stood in stunned silence.

Everyone that had stayed at the campfire now came pouring onto the scene; some wading waist deep while others came on the rafts. They were just in time to see Ben pick up Bold One's limp body and carry it slowly to the barn where he laid her in the hay. He wiped the tears from his face and walked back to the circle of people that were still all standing silently looking at the man on the ground.

"Who is he?" Someone finally asked. No one answered. They didn't know him. Most of them had not even known that he was there.

"He is probably a drifter," offered Tom. "Look one of the bullets hit him in the chest." People murmured but none of them seemed excessively upset by his death.

"He must have a horse hidden nearby. He didn't come with us," said Tom. The men spread out in the growing dark and soon discovered the horse up river, tied near the water, in a clump of trees not far from the place where the women had bathed. He was just out of sight of the camp.

Buddy had returned to the gate and stood there stomping his front feet, impatiently waiting to be let back into the corral. Ben walked over to him and hugged his neck and took him all the way into the barn, to his stall and gave him extra grain.

"See how special you are, Buddy. People even want to steal you." Ben struggled to untie the knots in the rope on Buddy's neck. He finally gave up and cut it off. "No one should tie a rope that tight on a horse's neck," he said in disgust. He walked over to each horse in the barn, giving each a special hug and pats or scratches. The big doors to the barn had stood open and the horses had gone in on their own. Maybe so many people walking past the corral bothered them, too. He picked up a shovel and cradled Bold One in his arms, ducking out to the backside of the barn; he couldn't help noticing the bullet holes in her, as he buried her. "That man was meant to die! A bullet passed through you and into him. You were very special, little Mama. We all loved you, Bold One, and will always remember you," he said. "Thank you for protecting me one last time."

Stump came and sat beside him and whined. Ben wasn't sure if Stump was giving comfort or receiving it but he sat on the ground and held the big brown and yellow dog in his arms for several minutes. He leaned the shovel against the wall of the barn and then carried the lantern down the path to the den. The pups were there, just outside the mouth of it, whining.

"Well, little guys, you are going to stay in the barn until all these people leave and I wish your dad would stay in there, too."

Ben carried them back and put them in the pen he had used for the chickens during the winter. He returned to the den to bring the basket of water.

"It's a good thing that you are weaned. I know that jerky was hard, but I'll get you something softer tomorrow morning." He closed the barn door as he left.

It seemed that no one had done anything while he was gone. The man was still lying where he had been. Everyone remained standing nearby. None had gone back across to the campfire.

"We know who he is," said Sam. "He is a drifter and a horse thief. What do you think of a guy that carries around his own wanted poster? We checked his saddle bags. There is a reward. I guess you could collect it. It was your wolf that killed him."

"I don't want any reward," said Ben. "Please, just someone, bury him away from here and I don't want him near my folk's grave by the big oak where we cross. Would someone take him up river, into the woods please?"

"I will. He extended his right hand. I'm Slim Parker. I'm the man that shot your wolf. I'm really sorry about her. I guess I just got scared. I'll take this "no good" out of here. Do you want me to take the wolf, too?"

"No. Thanks, I took care of that myself," said Ben. "That's where I was, when I walked away from here. I didn't want Beth to see her. The wolf was her special pet."

"I don't know what to say, I guess I can't say anything to fix it." Two men picked up the dead man and put him face down over the saddle of his own horse and slowly, Slim led the horse away.

Jed and Beth hurried to Ben's side.

"Ben we heard what happened! We heard the shots but we had gone back to the house. We started back here right away. It is so terrible! Are you all right?" Jed's face was lined with concern. Beth wrapped her arms around Ben's chest. Laying her head against him, she saw the blood on his shirt from carrying Bold One. He could feel her trembling. She was breathing hard from the fast walk and the stressful situation. He became concerned about her.

"I'm all right Beth, it's over now. He had Buddy and was leading him away when I saw him. He pulled a knife. It is still there on the ground." No one had touched it. Jed bent over and picked it up.

"This is my hunting knife! He must have taken it from the hut!"

"Oh Jed, he was a terrible man! But if Bold One hadn't killed him, she would still be alive, but Ben, then you might be dead! What a horrible thing to happen!" Tears slid down Beth's face as she realized that her beautiful wolf was gone.

"Where is she? I want to see her one last time."

"No Beth. Remember her as she was when you tamed her. I buried her."

"Where is he?" asked Jed. Calvin Briggs stepped up.

"Slim Parker has taken him up river to git him buried. Slim is the one that shot the wolf, and I saw that one of his bullets went in the man's chest."

"Here's the poster from his saddle bag." Jed read the poster and showed it to Beth.

"I met him earlier. He was in the hut. He said he was working on the ceiling over the boulder."

"He must have seen the fire and heard all the people and just rode in. How come nobody noticed him?"

"Maybe they did but they didn't know who he was and with so many new folks, they just thought he was from the settlement," offered Mathew Morgan.

"His name was John Gray. I talked to him earlier. He said he wanted to buy Buddy. I said no, he isn't for sale. When I caught him with Buddy on a rope, he said he wanted to take him for a trial ride. Anyone who knows and cares about horses would know that Buddy is too young to be ridden by a heavy man!" Ben sounded furious and hurt at the same time.

Quite a few minutes passed before Slim Parker returned leading the horse. People continued to stand around. Conversations were quiet and few.

"Is it all right if I put his horse in your barn and feed him? He doesn't look like he has been treated very well," said Slim.

"Sure, put him in one of the back stalls where he will be able to relax and not be bothered."

In a few minutes Ben followed Slim into the barn and checked on all the animals. He made sure that the drifter's horse had grain and water as well as fresh hay. Slim had given him everything that he needed. His saddle had been wiped clean of his owner's blood and oiled. It lay nearby on a pile of fresh hay. The leather was well worn, dry and scratched. He looked at the horse again and could see scars where he had been raked with spurs. Ben reached over and touched them and the horse shied away from him.

"No one will ever use spurs or a whip on you, ever again. You are safe here. Just rest and eat. I will see you in the morning." He slowly reached up and scratched the ears of the big horse. It was not until then that Ben realized just how large the horse was. He was taller than any horse Ben had ever ridden.

His father's horse, Dart Away, had been long legged with strong muscles but not this tall, and this horse had stronger looking muscles.

"At least you must have gotten enough to eat with all the wild grain. You don't look thin." He put a bar across the open end of the stall even though the horse was tied on a rope near the feed and water. It was more to make him feel protected than to pen him in.

Slim walked up to Ben in the circle of lantern light.

"He sure is a big one, isn't he? I can't say that I ever saw a saddle horse that big before." They stood there for a minute then Slim said that he was going over to the campfire and bring back some of the deer meat that was roasted for Stump and the pups. They will feel lonely tonight. No use their being hungry, too. He hurried out of the barn looking very sad.

Ben thought in spite of everything that had happened he liked Slim. He hoped that he would be a friend. Jed and Beth and most of the people had gone back to the campfire when Ben came out of the barn.

Someone had thoughtfully used a shovel and cleaned the area where the man had lain. The blood stain was gone. Ben felt grateful for that.

CHAPTER THREE   MELANIE BRIGGS

Melanie stepped out of the shadow of the trees with two cups of coffee.

"I hope you don't mind. I thought you might want to have a cup of coffee here where it is quiet, before you come back to the campfire. You must be very tired after all the hard work today, and then the events of this evening. Here let's sit on the grass and just rest."

She slid gracefully to the ground. Her full skirt spread out around her, giving the impression of an open rose. The glow of the moon filtered through the trees just enough so that he could see her cherub's face and the moonlit shine of her beautiful hair.

"I hope you don't think I'm being forward. My name is Melanie Briggs. I saw you talking to my father earlier today.

It is so lovely and quiet here. I could stay here forever." She sighed dramatically and sipped her cup of coffee, while Ben tried to stifle a yawn. He smiled at her and sipped the cup she had handed him.

"Everything here is so green," said Melanie. "It was terribly dry where we came from. Nothing would grow. We were so sad to leave the farm and my grandparents and uncle and aunt and my cousins are there, but they have a place like this, near a river."

"I hope your folks can find someplace nice that will grow things. I saw you helping with the garden today," said Ben. "I sure do appreciate everyone coming and helping the way they have."

"Ben, tell me about yourself," said Melanie "Where are you from? Family is so important."

"Melanie, my folks were killed by Indians just when my father picked this spot. The Indians took my sister, Sarah, with them. Someday when I can, I plan to go find her."

"So you have been here alone all that time?"

"Three years, but Jed has been here with me, after the first summer and then he married Beth and she is here too, with Johnny."

"It must have been dreadful for you. You have survived well. I wish that awful man had not come along to spoil things. People were having a wonderful time here until all that happened." She hesitated just a moment. "I hope I didn't make you sad, asking about your family."

"No Melanie, I am not sad, but I am tired and so are you. I think we better go back over and get some rest. I am glad you brought the coffee. You were right. I did need to just sit quietly for a few minutes. I enjoyed talking to you." He reached for her hand to help her up.

"Let's just stay here another minute," she said. He smiled and continued to hold her hand, as he led her carefully through the trees to his small raft that floated there. She turned to him and placed a soft hand on the chest of his leather shirt. It was still damp from being scrubbed.

"Ben, I hope you find your sister one day. When you do, I hope that she will come and live with you. She won't be the little girl you remember. I hope that it will be the way you want it. You shouldn't be alone."

He reached around her to loosen the rope to the raft and as he did, his arms encircled her. In that instant, she thought that she would like to stay in the protection of his strong arms. Of course he has to build me a house like Jed's, only bigger. I could never live in a house with dirt floors and covered over with more dirt. That's not for a civilized lady, she thought. I'm not being unrealistic. One must set high standards and have goals if they are to excel in life.

He helped her off the raft and up to the fire. People were still eating or sipping coffee. As they joined the group, Ben heard Melanie's mother scold her.

"Where have you been? It isn't proper for you to be off with that young man in the dark without an escort." He didn't hear her reply.

Ben was tired in every muscle of his body, but it wasn't from the work. It was a total weariness. The same kind he had felt after he had buried his folks. This has been a day that I will never forget, he thought. It hasn't been all bad though.

Thank you, Lord, for my protection today. Thank you for all the good people that are here. They were willing to travel here and work so hard for us. Everything is getting done at one time. I met Melanie. She is so sweet and beautiful. He thought about holding her hand as he drifted off to sleep.

39

Melanie was having trouble quieting her mind so she could go to sleep. She prayed for the soul of the man that had died. She wondered if he had anyone that would ever miss him. She was the only one that prayed for him.

"For the sake of your name, O Lord, forgive my iniquity, though it is great. Who, then, are those who fear the Lord? He will instruct them in the ways they should choose. They will spend their days in prosperity, and their descendants will inherit the land." Psalm 25 11-13 NIV "Forgive him Lord."

She prayed for her parents and asked that they find a place as good as Ben's land near a river or a lake. She thanked God for the chance to meet Ben. She thought that he was the most handsome man she had ever met. She liked his darkly tanned skin against his long wavy blond hair. She liked the sparkle in his blue eyes. She was remembering how Ben had looked in the firelight when Jed held Johnny up and introduced him. She asked God to bless and comfort him as she fell asleep.

The strange sounds of many people working on his house woke Jed. He had not fallen asleep until it was nearly morning. Beth too, had slept fitfully and looked tired as she sat near the morning fire nursing Johnny. Gentle Fawn had already fed the twins and sat beside Beth in friendly companionship.

"When our man is upset we do not sleep well."

"I am a bit tired this morning," said Beth, "but I am also excited about the new house. I can't wait to move in. Jed and Ben said they would work at making furniture as time allows. I will make some curtains from the white cotton I have. Sam said they are going to use lumber to plank the floor! It will be like a real house." Gentle Fawn smiled.

"Do you miss the house you left to come here?"

"No not at all. Jed and Ben have been so good to me and they have worked very hard to make things as nice for us as they could. It hasn't been easy for them. I do miss little things, like shoes that fit my feet and dresses that are soft and pretty."

"The brown dress you had on when we arrived was pretty. Did you make it?" "Yes. I used the husks from the hickory nuts to dye it dark. Jed cut the circles of bone for decorations on the sleeves. He made the first dress I had from leather. The cotton one I was wearing when they found me was all I had to wear for a whole year! It was dirty, torn and worn out. I like wearing leather in the cold months. It feels good. The wind can't go through it," said Beth.

The women had finished up their quick morning chores and were ready to cross the river.

"You go with them. Let me keep Johnny here with me. He and the twins will sleep now for a while anyway," said Gentle Fawn. "Because he is smaller, he will wake sooner and get hungry again before you return, May I feed him?" Beth smiled at her and hugged her whispering, "Thank you. You are a most precious friend." Beth joined the group of waiting ladies.

The Land's Heritage

They settled themselves in a giggly colorful mass in the middle of the big raft that had been used to bring the lumber across. Sam and Matthew Morgan pulled it across. Ropes had been attached to trees and to the four corners to make the job easy and help stabilize the raft. They could pull it from the bank in either direction without getting wet. Each lady had a bundle in her arms, held tightly and protected from the least drop of water.

Once safe and dry on the other side of the river they hurried to the garden, ready to get it planted. Helen's large bundle contained seed potatoes. Another had red apple seeds held tightly in a handkerchief. They planted the apple seeds in the corners and marked the spots with sticks they had stripped of bark. They followed Beth's plan for putting the peppers closer to the middle so they would get the benefit of more sun. Sweet corn was put in rows in the center. The shorter plants were put nearer the fence so that the deer and elk couldn't reach anything.

On the right went the cabbage and potatoes and on the left they planted carrots, beets, and parsnips. The popcorn was in hills and so were the potatoes. Marigolds separated the cabbage and tomatoes. The squash went along one end and the pumpkins along the other. By the time they were finished, Beth admitted she wasn't sure where everything was, but hoped that she would recognize them after they sprouted.

Ben wandered over to see how the women were getting on with the job, to find they were almost finished. The ground had been planted in various hills and rows, but no plants would be there unless God blessed it with a gentle rain when needed. I think this huge garden would be very difficult to water from the lake, he thought. I will do it if it is necessary.

"How are they doing on the house?" asked a very friendly looking lady with brown hair, green eyes and a big smile.

"It is coming along really well," answered Ben. "They have started to put the uprights, where the doors will be. Matthew Morgan is making metal hinges. He is using some of the metal parts I had in the barn. That's his pounding that you hear," said Ben.

"It sounds almost like a small bell," said Mary.

"Maybe he can make a bell for us when we build a real church."

"Lizzy that's a good idea!" exclaimed Melanie's mother, Minnie. She was very round and red faced from bending over in the garden. Beads of perspiration dotted her forehead and her plump arms attempted to cover the wet rings beneath them. Her dress tucked in beneath her more than ample breasts and spread out from there to cover her ankles like an umbrella.

"When will you be building the church?" asked Ben.

"Oh, I don't know. It won't be soon. It is still just a bee in a few folk's bonnets," Helen answered.

"If I know about it, I will come and help," offered Ben.

"Child it looks to me like you have plenty here to keep you busy. I hope you know how much work a garden this size is going to be. Weeding alone is going to break your back the first few years until you get the soil cleaned of most of the weed roots," said Rose.

"Ben, have you met all these ladies?"

"No I haven't. I was embarrassed to say so." The plump lady's eyes twinkled.

"I'm Melanie's mother, Minnie. I know you have met her." Melanie giggled.

"Hello," she said.

"Next is Lizzy. She is Matt Morgan's wife. They have two girls running around here somewhere. They are the two with the long blond braids. Over here is Mary. She is Slim Parker's wife. They have two boys. That one is hers," she pointed at a baby boy asleep on a blanket in the shade, "also they have a bigger one. He is probably over with his father where the men are. The one in blue over there is Sue Ellen. She's Ezra's wife. He works at the mill for Tom."

"It is nice to meet all of you. I appreciate all your hard work. Thank you so much for coming here and helping. I think I better go over to the hill now. Matt and I are going hunting as soon as he finishes the last hinge."

Matt was on his way down the path by the lake when Ben came around the bend.

"You ready to go hunting?" asked Ben.

"I sure am," answered Matt. "My horse is over there under the trees. I tied him where there was grass so he could graze. Why don't you try out that big one?" Ben didn't want to admit it but it had been a long time since he had ridden on a horse with a saddle. He wasn't sure that he could do it well enough for riding and hunting with someone. As he walked to the barn he decided it was best to say so.

"I have not ridden since all the horses were taken from our wagon. My dad had a beautiful saddle horse, but they took him. I hope this big guy is easy to ride."

"Just like sitting in a rocking chair Ben." Matthew laughed heartily as they entered the barn. "That young fella that Gray was trying to steal is sure a beauty. Have you started to train him yet?"

"No, not much, but we have had him carrying a light weight on his back a few times. He has a high spirit and I want him to let me ride rather than force him to carry me."

"That's good. It does take patience. I can't stand to see folks misuse their animals."

The big brown horse was eyeing them warily with its ears held back. Ben picked up the saddle and started toward him, then laid it back down.

"Maybe I should introduce myself first," he said with a little nervous chuckle. "You are a wonderful big boy. Yes you are." Ben scratched the horse's ears and neck and chest and worked at making friends. He quickly peeked at his front teeth. "He isn't real old. What is your name, big brown boy?"

"Hey did you see his ears perk up when you said that?" asked Matt. "I think his name might be big boy, or something close to that," said Matt.

"Is that your name? Are you Big Boy?" The horse nudged Ben's hand with his muzzle.

"He sure likes being scratched," said Matt. Ben picked up the saddle a second time and placed it on top of a blanket on the horses back. His head came around and he tried to bite Ben.

"Hey, Big Boy, I was just going to ride you! I don't own spurs or a whip. Now let's try this again." Matt was laughing so hard, that he was no help at all. When Ben turned to tighten the cinch, the horse tried to bite him again.

"No you don't," said Ben. He was ready for him. He stuffed a wad of fresh hay in the horse's mouth. Big Boy looked totally surprised.

Both men turned toward the pup pen when they heard a giggle. Melanie stood there with Sunshine in her arms and a smile on her face.

"I hope you don't mind me being in here. I was thinking of the poor little guys being lonely without their mother and I came in to play with them for a few minutes. You better be careful with that beast! He is awfully big and looks like he could be rather difficult."

"Thanks for checking on the pups. I'll try not to get hurt."

When Ben looked back at the horse he could see that wasn't at all what he expected. Big Boy chewed the bite of hay and stood still as Ben got on and off twice.

"What do you think Matt?"

"I think you have a lot of horse there, and if you work with him, you're going to love him. He just needs to learn to respect and trust you." Ben noticed a rifle in its sleeve on the saddle. "I'm glad to have an extra rifle but I think I'll use my own today." The drifter's rifle was unloaded and hooked high on the wall of the hut out of the children's reach and Ben came out with his own gun. He placed it in the sleeve and almost felt comfortable with Big Boy, as he led him out of the barn and mounted for the third time.

Matt strolled over to his horse and swung up with the ease of familiarity. The two men headed out across the river, away from the camp and the chuck wagon and out onto the prairie.

They moved at a slow pace at first, until Matt suggested that they give the horses a little run. Big Boy didn't need much encouragement to speed past Matt and way out in front. Ben reined him in and noticed that he was not even warm.

"This horse would be good for a long journey. He is not easily tired."

"He runs like fury," said Matt, "like he could do it all day!"

Ben breathed a prayer of thanksgiving to God for a horse that could take him on a journey to find Sarah. The two had been well entertained but they really were not doing much in the way of hunting.

"We better find us some game or that hungry crew back there will be pretty cross, come evening," Matt said.

"There is dust over there, let's go see what is stirring it up." They moved at a steady pace until they reached the top of a slight rise, where they stopped to look.

The dust was from a herd of horses. Ben recognized the stallion.

"That's the same herd that I took my horses from," said Ben. "We will have to be alert after everyone leaves. That stallion hasn't been around for a while. He may try again to get them back. It's good to have the knowledge that he is in the area."

They headed toward the river and trees. There in the quiet shaded brush they saw a large deer. Ben shot and without warning, he was unseated. Big Boy instantly reared and bolted. He went tearing down the prairie as if his tail was on fire. Ben lit hard on the prairie sod. The wind was knocked out of him. It all happened so fast that he wasn't sure what had happened. Matt was laughing again.

"Well Ben, now, you know that he doesn't like you to shoot a gun from his back. I'll go see if I can catch up with him. Are you hurt?" Ben shook his head no as he dusted off his trousers and felt around for anything broken and then he made sure that his rifle was not damaged. This was not like sitting in a rocking chair, he thought!

"Guess I'll live! It would help if you weren't enjoying it so much!" Then Ben joined in the laughter.

"Good, you can start working on that deer. You are a good shot Ben." Matt headed out in the direction that Big Boy had taken. He was standing near the river munching grass when Matt found him. He offered no resistance when Matt picked up his reins and led him back to Ben.

It took both men using Matt's horse, to lift the deer with a rope they had tossed over a branch for leverage. They settled it behind the saddle on Big Boy. They had fastened his reins securely to a tree, just in case he decided he wouldn't stand there to have the deer loaded on his back. He nibbled grass and acted like nothing unusual had happened until Ben mounted. As soon as he was freed, and Ben had settled in the saddle, he reared up trying to unseat Ben again. This time Ben held his seat. He was ready for him. He didn't scold. He talked softly and patted and scratched him.

They arrived back at camp just as the campfire was getting fed to build it up for some serious cooking. Ben could see two big pots filled with water and beans near the fire and another by the wagon had dough rising in it.

"Looks like we will be having another feast tonight," he said. The deer was skinned and then they helped the cook get the huge animal over the fire. They talked with him asking what he would do when he returned to the village, knowing that he was one of the new arrivals.

"Folks call me Cookie I like telling stories. I guess sometimes they get a bit long. I will be opening a restaurant, with steaks, and fried potatoes mostly. I'll make eggs for breakfast. I brew my own spirits and as soon as I get established, you and your family are invited for a free meal."

"Well we appreciate the offer, but we should be feeding you. You have been working here cooking ever since you rolled in."

"This is a vacation compared to what I need to do when I get back. I gave a few seed potatoes to the women so they could plant them in your garden. I plan on putting in an acre of them when we get back. Then while they are growing I have a restaurant to build, with a back room to sleep in. I need to be in business with the chuck wagon, to make money for supplies. Folks here are a blessing, and I know that they will help when I need it. I'll have wild grain for whisky, wild grapes for wine, and I plan on trying my hand at some beer later on.

"Cookie, it is nice to know your name and I guess you already know ours. He is Matt Morgan, a blacksmith and I'm Ben Slater. We best get over to the house now, maybe we will get a chance to visit later."

"He does rattle on some," said Matt with a chuckle when they were far enough away that Cookie couldn't hear the comment.

While Gentle Fawn had been relieved of the babies she had been out on the prairie gathering dandelion greens. She had several big basketfuls down by the river washing the dust from them. She saw the size of the deer they had brought in, and praised their hunting skills.

"Ben, will you allow me to scrape the hide for you?"

"Thank you Gentle Fawn, but wouldn't you rather go visit with the women while you can?"

"I like to visit, but I will stake the skin in the shade with Beth nearby. We will have a talk. I will have to leave when the house is done. I wish you all lived near the settlement."

It is sad, thought Ben, that she is more comfortable here than with the other ladies. I wonder if she is lonely in the settlement.

Beth sat on a blanket watching Stormy developing dexterity as he played with a twig with leaves on it. Ann made happy sounds and reached for a colorful gourd rattle that Beth held out. Johnny was cuddled close, sleeping. They both smiled at her but didn't speak when they came near. She smiled back not wanting to wake Johnny.

"Matt, did you notice that Big Boy didn't seem to mind the water at all? Ginger is used to it now and I didn't think about it when we left. He just tromped through as if it were part of the path. He is quite a good horse. It is sad that he was so mistreated."

"Yes, it will take work to overcome the quirks he has developed because of it. I noticed you stuffed his mouth with hay when he tried to bite you. That was a good start. You may have to be ready to do that for a while."

"Let's go see how the house is coming," said Matt.

After removing the saddle, Ben put Big Boy in the corral and watched as he nosed the other horses getting acquainted. Ben grinned at the way he sidled up to Ginger and rubbed his muzzle on her back.

"He doesn't waste any time does he?" said Matt.

"Do you think he might hurt her, should I take him out of there?"

"No, I don't think he will harm her. He is just getting acquainted."

The house had all four walls up and the roof beams silhouetted against the sky. Jed walked over smiling from ear to ear.

"Isn't it wonderful? By tomorrow night they will have it closed in and the windows and doors in." Ben was smiling. He was so happy for Jed and Beth. "It has wood plank floors! They already have the partition walls for the bedrooms up inside. Look in there."

For Jed, it was Christmas. Ben rather felt like that also. The men were watching Jed and enjoying his enthusiasm.

Calvin came over and said that they had pulled over enough rock for a big fireplace and chimney.

"Most of them came right out of the water. They are going to have to dry out slowly or they will burst," he said.

"You sound like you have had that experience," said Jed.

"It's easy to get impatient when you see it all put together. Folks want to see a big fire in their new fireplace. That's when the rocks bust. You have to start with a fire the size of a barn cat and just keep that going several days. Then you can increase it very slowly."

"I will be sure to remember that," said Jed. "We will be starting to put it together in the morning, we can use some help, to hand the rocks in the window, if you're willing."

"Glad to," said Matt.

"Count on me," said Ben and Jed at the same time, and then laughed.

The women had been working all afternoon piecing together a quilt of hand decorated blocks. Nearly every lady in the settlement had made at least one block. Each block was unique.

"We will not have time to hand quilt the whole thing by the time the men are finished. Do you think it would be good if we tie it with this yarn? I brought it along, just in case." offered Helen.

"That should be fine. It will be pretty and hold together well," said Rose. "We could start quilting the middle and when we start running out of time, we could just tie the edges."

"Let's do that," said Lizzy. "I have one done like that and it has held up through years of use." The women agreed that it was a good solution.

They were working under the edge of the trees near the wolf den. They liked the soft bed of grass under the huge old pines. From there they had a view of the garden they had planted, part of the lake and the hill beyond, where the men were working.

"It really is starting to look like a house," said Helen as she glanced up from her stitching. She handed her needle to Minnie and stood on the path when she saw Beth coming. She couldn't wait another minute to go check the progress. Helen didn't feel comfortable going to the hill without someone with her.

Jed saw them coming and went to meet them.

"Hello, ladies." he laughed. "Have you come to help finish the roof?" Both women laughed with him. Jed hugged Beth and swung her around.

"I can't believe how fast this house is going up," said Helen.

"They are doing the fireplace and the roof today. By tonight they will have the windows and doors in," he said. "Honey, can you believe how fast this house has gone together?"

"It is amazing! Come on Jed, we want to go inside," she responded. They walked through the rooms and Beth looked at everything making comments. When they stepped out onto the grass, she saw that two men seemed to be making boxes.

"What are you making?" She asked. "Cupboards," said one. "A set of shelves for the wall by the fireplace," answered the other.

"Oh everything is so wonderful!" she said. Jed had to read her lips because the pounding on the roof echoed and drowned out her words.

Ben smiled as he handed a rock from the pile selected by Calvin the day before, to Matthew. He in turn took the rock a few steps and placed it beside Calvin who was fitting them expertly into a growing facade for the chimney.

"Once this has time to dry and set it will be here for your great grandbabies," Calvin said.

"It looks beautiful already, with all the different colors in the rocks," said Ben.

"River rock is the best, when you can get it," replied Calvin.

Two men continued to work on improving and shoring up the tunnel. Dirt was being handed out on both ends and boards were slid in to brace the ceiling so that it would not collapse.

"That is like being in a small mine," said one of the men as he crawled out. "It is a great idea though, to have a way to leave the house that the Indians can't see. We put the mouth way back there behind the pines and we have dug a few holes on all sides back from it and transplanted some small pines. Jed, you will need to remember to carry water to them until they get going. That way the exit will be covered from all directions."

"That's so good. You can be sure that I won't forget."

Jed walked Beth and Helen back to the group of ladies.

"That is the prettiest quilt I have ever seen, ladies. You have so many talents. I can't wait to see things start growing in that garden you planted. They smiled and one commented that the first thing he would see would probably be weeds.

"We had to work hard on pulling weeds last year, but it sure is worth it." He continued up the path to the corral where he tossed big bundles of hay in for the horses, and opened the trench to fill the small pond. I am guessing that Ben's new big horse eats a lot. He stood watching the horses until it was filled then put the slate and rock back in place.

When he left, Rusty was once again stomping around in the middle of the pond. Big Boy quickly buried his face in the fresh hay and came up with a huge mouthful. Jed suddenly realized, the youngest horse we have is Surprise and he is nearly a year old! I am glad that none of them are old enough for the big fella to recognize them as competition for the ladies in there. They wouldn't stand a chance.

When things settle down I think we need to start some serious training on you guys, Jed thought. He went in the barn and stepped into the pen with the pups to check that they had food and water.

He sat down and played with them for a few minutes. Sunshine crawled up on him and tried to lick his face.

"Beth has been allowing that hasn't she?" He tickled tummies and scratched behind ears a little more and saw that they needed something to entertain them. Rascal pulled hard on the fringe of his shirt sleeve, breaking off a strand of leather. "No you rascal, she named you right. My shirt is not to play with." He tossed in a piece of soft leather that hung on the wall.

"There you go, chew on that." He could hear a tug of war going on as he left the barn. Stump came up to him wagging his tail. His mouth held a huge bone from the leg of the deer. Jed watched as Stump went in the barn and sailed easily over the contrived wall of the pen to visit his pups and provide them with a treat.

CHAPTER FOUR   THE LAST NAIL

As the sun lowered in the sky the tiniest of smoke curls could be seen coming from the new chimney. Tom was still on the roof pounding nails into the last few wooden roof shingles, while others were gathering up scraps of wood and making a neat pile near the woods behind the house. The windows were in and opened wide. The door was on and stood open on a porch wide enough for several chairs. A bucket of dry sand had been poured on the floors of the new house and music from an accordion drifted across the lake.

A big fire was lit near the lake and quilts and blankets in bright colors ringed it. The cooked food was ferried over and ready. When the last nail went in, a loud cheer went up.

Everyone gathered around as Jed and Beth entered their completed new house for the first time. Jed swept Beth into his arms and carried her through the living room and stood her up in the middle of their empty bedroom. His action was met with catcalls and whistles mixed with joyous laughter. After Jed's lingering kiss, Beth's face was bright red as she quickly returned to the front doorway, looking at all their wonderful friends.

She took Johnny into her arms and thanked Rose and Gentle Fawn for taking such good care of him for hours at a time the past few days. She carried him into his new bedroom and turned in a circle.

"This is your room Johnny, all yours until you have a little brother or sister." He cooed and tangled his little fingers in her hair, quite happy just to be back in her arms.

As the kettles of food and baskets of plates and necessary items were placed by the fire, happy voices filled the air.

Helen, Gentle Fawn and Rose stood up next to the fire and held up the finished quilt for all to see.

"We hope that you will be warm and cozy with this over you," said Rose. Oooo's and ahs and comments from some of the men that hadn't seen it made the women feel they had done a beautiful job. Beth and Jed thanked them all profusely.

Laughter mixed with the music as people filled their plates. Sam stood and asked God to bless this new home and the family that would live there.

"Bless them going in and bless them coming out, Lord," he said. "We thank you, Father for watching over all of us, while it was built. We thank you for the abundance we have been given so that we can share with Jed and Beth. We ask you to continue to bless Ben, and to give all of us a safe journey home and bless the food in Jesus' mighty name," and everyone loudly said, "Amen!" Jed stood up to speak but he was so moved with emotion that his throat was tight and he had trouble speaking.

"Thank you, so much. We love all of you. Thank you." Applause filled the air and he sat down.

"Let's eat before the food gets cold," said Minnie and everyone started talking, while filling their plates.

Beth reached over and placed her hand on Jed's arm.

"Jed we have a home. A new beautiful house is standing right there and it is for us! I see it but it feels like a dream. I still can't believe it!"

"This is a dream Beth, a dream come true," replied Jed. He took a bite of the deer meat and looked over at the back of the lake.

"Where do you think we should build our barn?"

"Jed, I don't believe it! Can't you give yourself one day of rest, before you think up another big project? Well you have to rest soon. Tomorrow is Saturday. You have one day and then Sunday you will rest, whether you like it or not!" She tried to sound stern, but couldn't help laughing when she said it. The accordion music started up again, and people were drifting into the house.

"What are they doing in there?" asked Beth.

"Come on and I'll show you," he said, as he put their plates on the grass and handed the baby to Minnie Briggs.

"Jed, you can't just hand Johnny off like he is a bag of seed!"

"She already said she wanted to hold him."

"Jed!"

When they stepped through the front door, every room had couples dancing and turning.

"This is how the floor gets sanded," he said as he held her closely and swayed to the music. You don't want to get a splinter in your feet some night, do you? We need to help, he laughed as Sam went whirling past with Helen laughing loudly." She noticed that once in a while someone would push sand into a corner and move it back and forth with their foot.

"By late tonight every inch of the floor will be smooth."

"This is a fun way to do a hard job," she giggled as he waltzed her into the corner of their bedroom and kissed her tenderly.

"I can see that we are going to need a door on here," she said with a smile.

As the men and women grew tired from dancing, they drifted back to the fire and sat on the blankets. A close companionship bonded the group with love and a shared faith in God and their future. Ben had been dancing with Melanie and they seemed oblivious to anyone else around them.

Now they sat holding hands on the grass, at the edge of the light from the fire.

"I will come down river this fall. I promise, Melanie. It will be a long summer," he said. "I will miss you."

"I will miss you too. I wish we didn't have to leave in the morning, but my parents plan on building a house on the Silver River before winter," Melanie continued, "I hope it is as nice as this one. This house feels like a warm hug when I walk in."

"Melanie I love you. Will you marry me?"

"Marry you? Oh, my Ben! I don't know!"

"Now, this fall or whenever you want."

"Ben I have known you such a short time. My head tells me that I should wait, but my heart is telling me something else," Melanie paused and then said, "Do you really want to marry me? You don't really know me. I have a terrible temper and my mother says that I am willful, and…"

"Yes I really want to marry you!"

"Oh Ben, I think I love you. I know I have strong feelings for you. I think I will marry you but I need to…and her voice trailed off"

"When," he asked?

"In a month or two the preacher will be coming back to the settlement. Helen told me that. Let's do it then. That would mean I will have to wait all summer, but that way you can help your parents get settled."

"That's hardly the way to court a girl."

"I know, but then we will be together the rest of our lives."

"I feel I do have to stay with my folks, Ben, to help until they get settled in a new place. It won't be that long. We will both be busy. You can come see me whenever you want now that all the work is done."

"Melanie, I want to. You are so beautiful, but you must realize that the work here is never going to be done. If you will marry me we can raise lots of horses and have a large family and maybe someday we could have a house like Jed's."

"Someday? Well Ben, I am so flattered that you want me, but we must take the summer and spend lots of time together visiting in town and see what the lovely future brings."

Ben was so happy that he felt like shouting! He wasn't listening to her words at all.

"Hey everybody, Melanie just said she would marry me!" A frown crossed Melanie's face for an instant and then a bright smile took its place. She loved being the center of attention, but that wasn't what she had said.

Everyone was congratulating them and smiling and laughing, everyone except her father and mother.

"You should have asked them first. My father is upset," said Melanie. Ben walked over to Calvin and Minnie and apologized for not asking them first. He explained that he knew he had been impulsive but he had just asked her and was so happy that it just came out! He just had to tell everyone!

"You will have her for all summer. I want to get married before the preacher leaves the settlement in the fall." Her parents relented and hugged him warmly and they were hugging and being hugged by everyone. Melanie was beaming.

Beth was delighted by the news. The only sad thing about having the new house was that they would be leaving Ben alone. Now he would have a wife to plan for and to keep him company next winter and for the years to come. Jed wasn't thinking that at all. He was thinking that Melanie had Ben dancing on a string.

Melanie lay in her blankets that night very troubled. I just don't know how that young man thinks. I told him plain as day that I needed to be courted. He just blurted out we were going to be married. What was I to do? He didn't even have a ring to offer me. I don't know what I will do. This is very embarrassing. I know I have got to do something.

In the morning everything that had been disturbed by the activities of so many people was tidied and put in the best possible order. All their tools, cooking pots, and kettles were back on the wagons. Water bags were filled and supplies and blankets put onto the wagons for the long trip home. Goodbyes, were said, along with hugs and a few tears. All of the people had hopped onto one wagon or another unless they were in a saddle. With the loads of lumber and building supplies gone, the strong work horses would have an easy job pulling the wagons back to the settlement. Ben held Melanie's hand until the wagons had started to move and then he lifted her up onto the blankets in the last wagon. Jed stepped close to Ben as they watched the wagons pull away.

"She is a beauty," he said. "She could turn any man's head and remove his common sense."

"Thanks Jed, I sure think so." Ben hadn't really heard Jed's statement either. He was still focusing on Melanie's smile and wave from the back of the wagon. He was in love for the first time in his life.

Ben, Jed and Beth watched the wagons leave, carrying the people of the settlement in the direction of their homes. When the wagons were so far away that individuals could not be discerned, Ben and Jed pulled the small raft across the Hickory with Beth and Johnny on it.

Their wonderful house that the settlement had just built still didn't seem quite real to Beth as she carefully stepped up the river bank with the baby in her arms and Jed's protective arm around her. As she looked back at the place where so many people had camped, she saw very little signs that they had been there. Only the patch of black ashes and dirt was there where the fire had been and the grass in the area was trampled. The first good rain would heal the grass and Jed had commented that he would go back with the shovel to cover the ashes with dirt. For a moment a wave of loneliness swept over her.

Jed announced that he and Ben had a few things to do.

"I am going to the hut to fix us something to eat, said Beth. They left us tons of food. Will you be long?" she asked.

"We need to do something over at the house, so hold off for a few minutes, if you don't mind." Jed headed for the barn with Ben beside him. They let the pups out of the pen and watched as they scampered around sniffing everything.

Jed handed parts of the new bed down the ladder to Ben.

"It sure is beautiful, Jed. You really did a great job on this," said Ben.

I can't wait until she sees it all set up in our bedroom!" The wood was heavy enough that it took two trips to get the pieces to the house. They weren't sure which direction to turn the headboard, but they figured it really didn't matter because she probably would want to move it anyway. Jed went out to the scrap pile and brought in planks to put across. They covered them with fresh hay and then two hides.

"All it needs is real bedding. I have feathers, lots and lots of feathers, from every duck, and bird we ever had. Beth can use them to make pillows and a mattress," said Ben.

"That's great," said Jed.

They hurried up the path to the hut. She was sitting in the shade with Johnny on her lap.

"I have something to show you," said Jed. "I am going to take Johnny's cradle over and put it in his room. Come with me," said Jed. "Ben, would you bring Beth's rocking chair?"

"Glad to," he said, hurrying in to get it. He wanted to be there when she saw the beautifully carved new bed.

They walked down the path, made wide by all the use. She went with him into Johnny's room and watched as he put the cradle near the wall. She laid the baby in it and smiled when he looked around realizing that he was in a different place.

"You are in your new room," she whispered. Ben put the rocker down near the window in the main room so she could sit and look out at the lake. Jed took her hand and led her into their bedroom.

"Jed! You made this! It is as beautiful as the cradle! When did you have time? The carving is so perfect. I love it!" She hugged him, and started to cry. He was totally puzzled.

"Why are you crying?"

"Because, I am so happy!" she wailed.

"Women," he said, and they all laughed.

"Ben and I have been planning to make some willow chairs for the living room area and a table and benches for there in the kitchen part. Which do you want us to do first?"

"I don't care, I am so happy, I feel like I have the whole world already!"

"Chairs it is," said Jed. He walked over and opened and closed the cupboard doors.

"I'll be glad when these are full of goodies," he said.

"Jed, look!" On a shelf above the little counter was a row of tins. The biggest held flour, the next sugar, the next coffee and the smallest one had English tea with a tiny strainer tucked in the top. Inside the lid was a note from Sam and Helen signed with love.

"They are all so wonderful!" she sobbed.

"There she goes again," said Ben smiling.

"Let's go get your bedding and then we can start cutting willow branches while she calms down. He hugged her as he slipped passed and out the door.

"Before we go, let's take a minute to thank God for this house and our friends and just everything," said Jed. They held hands and Jed gave God the thanks and praise that he felt in his heart. Ben added a prayer asking God to bless the new house and their friends on the journey back to the settlement.

"We should bring in some wood to keep that little fire going."

"Let's cut it into small pieces out there. I plan on making a box of birch, with the white bark to put it in, later on," said Jed. "I was thinking about how you made your bins for the hickory nuts, Ben. They look nice."

They each took in an armload of small branches. Jed carefully added a measured amount to the glowing coals.

"We have to keep it small. We don't want any of the rocks busting."

"Calvin is definitely a craftsman. That is the nicest fireplace I have ever seen," said Beth.

"Beth you can add some wood to it once in a while, but it is important that the fire stays small."

"Yes I know," she said, "Calvin told me."

She was thinking that she would try to make a large grass rug for the area by the windows, and that she wanted to make curtains.

Beth picked up Johnny and returned to Ben's hut and fixed a sandwich for each of them. She got a water bag and filled it with cool fresh water. She was able to coax the pups to follow her down the path, but when they got as far as the den they darted in and wouldn't follow her, the rest of the way.

"You are still waiting for your mother, aren't you? You poor little guys, she isn't coming back," she said tearfully. She knelt down and hugged them. "I miss her too," she said quietly as she turned to leave. Beth had loved Bold One very much. She couldn't stop the tears that slid down her cheeks.

She had Johnny and the pouch with the sandwiches and the water bag. She couldn't carry them, but she wanted to. She stopped by the garden for a moment and still felt amazed at the progress their whole area had made in just the few short days that the people of the settlement had been there.

She circled the lake and found the men sitting down drawing with a stick in the dirt.

"What are you doing?" she asked.

"This is the house." Jed pointed to an X in the dirt. "This is the tree line." He pointed to a bunch of little dots. "This is the lake," which he had represented by a circle filled with wavy lines.

"Over there we will build the barn, and the corral can cut through the trees and the fence will circle back to the edge of the lake and then over to the corner of the barn. He followed the line he had drawn with his finger. "This spot is where we plan to dig the well. What do you think, Beth?"

"I think you don't know how to take one day to relax and enjoy what we already have!"

He ignored her remark and continued planning.

"Beth, would you like me to dig you a flower bed near the house?"

"That would be a good idea for next year," she said. "We have planted all the seeds in the vegetable garden for this year. The marigolds are between the tomato plants, the poppies on this end and the sunflowers on the other," she recited with joy at the fact that the whole garden had been planted.

"We will let that wait until next spring," said Jed as he continued to study his drawing in the dust.

"Jed and I have been cutting willow for the chairs. The whole other side of the lake is ringed with willow trees. That will make it easy to build the fence for the corral," said Ben.

"They left enough wood to start the barn and after we drag all the trees that we had cut and cleaned for the cabin, we will still need to cut more, but not so many."

As he said that, Ben looked up to see Slim Parker and his wife Mary walk around the bend in the path with their two boys.

"Hello again," called Slim. "We have made a decision and are happy about it. We stopped to share it with you, before we go on." Beth greeted the little family with a big smile and a hug for Mary. Ben extended his hand to Slim and Jed was just a little surprised that Ben was so friendly with this man after what had happened earlier in the week.

"When I was talking with Ben the other night, I thought that it would be nice to live nearby where we could get to be real good friends," said Slim.

"Beth and Mary like each other and that baby of Beth's will soon be big enough to play with our boys, so we figured if we went down river a bit we could probably find us a spot that feels like home." Ben stood there with a foolish grin on his face. He was happy to hear that they wanted to be near and be friends.

"That is such good news! We will be happy to help you any way we can." Ben had forgiven Slim for shooting Bold One. Slim had reacted out of fear for his wife and sons. They all understood that.

After a little lunch and a lot of talk, Ben and Slim rode out up river. They traveled around the first bend and on beyond a second that Ben had not been aware of.

"None of this soil looks like it is good for crops, just yellow hard clay. I think we should go back and try down river from Jed's," said Slim.

They headed back along the river and followed it down stream until they reached the spot where Jed and Ben had caught the horses. He explained how they had made a surround; using Ginger tied at the back to coax the wild stallion to bring his herd into the water.

"That's how I got Buddy," said Ben. "He was just a foal then." Ben told Slim about seeing the spring in the woods nearby and the small band of Indians there.

"We will have to check that out, but I think this spot has lots of promise. Look at the rich color of the soil and how tall the grass is," said Slim. He was excited. "The ground looks like yours Ben. Yes sir, I like this spot. Where is that spring?" Ben felt uneasy.

"We need to be quiet along here until we see if there are Indians camped in there. Our voices carry a long way in the trees," said Ben.

They tied their horses just inside the tree line and Slim smiled at the sound of the bubbling water. Ben pulled his rifle from its sleeve and walked slowly in the direction of the spring, followed by Slim. He crouched in the bushes when he got near enough to see the small pool. Slim did the same.

"The only prints I can see are animal," said Slim. "I think you are right, let's go up the path and look around." Ben bent low and followed the path around the trees to the clearing that had held the communal fire circled by several tents. It was empty now. The fire pit was empty of ashes and the rocks around it had caught blown leaves and dried forest rubble. The entire area looked like it hadn't had a human foot on it for a long time.

"Thank God, said Slim, I'm going to hurry back to the settlement and file on this piece before someone else does!"

"What are you talking about?" asked Ben.

"You know what I mean. You have to get a paper at the registrar's office that says you are homesteading on your land. It's a paper that says it's yours or someone else can claim it and all your hard work is for nothing," said Slim.

"I haven't got a paper," said Ben. "I didn't know I had to do it."

"Well you better come with us and get one right away; you and Jed too!" said Slim.

"How could something like this happen? Someone like that man that tried to steal Buddy could come along and get a paper saying our place belongs to him?" asked Ben.

Ben felt sick. He urged the big horse into a gallop; wanting to get back quickly. He had to talk to Jed right away. Jed could tell with one look that something was upsetting Ben. His face was white as a sheet.

"What's the matter? Did you have trouble? Ben what is it?"

"This place and yours, we don't own them. They aren't ours. Anyone can claim them!"

"What are you talking about?" asked Beth. Slim says that we have to go to the settlement to the land office and get a paper that says this place is ours or someone else can claim it. It would legally be theirs! He said it's something new called the Homestead Act."

"Calm down Ben, I already knew about it. I have something for you," said Jed. He walked into the hut and from a niche in the wall; Jed pulled a small leather pouch. "Here, I planned to give you this when you turn twenty-one, but since you know about it already, you may as well see it so you will stop worrying." Ben's hands were shaking as he opened the paper. He read every word.

"This describes this place and the map shows that it includes more than half way across the lake but it's in Beth's name," said Ben.

"I had to think fast when we were there. They only allow one hundred and sixty acres per person. You would not be eligible to sign for a homestead until you are twenty-one. So I put Beth's name on it to hold it until you are."

"So I don't own any of this? My place belongs to Beth?" Ben's face was drawn tight with emotion.

"Yes legally, but it isn't as if she was trying to take it from you. She didn't even know that I did it."

"Jed this isn't fair! It isn't right at all! This whole thing is wrong! Someone could come along and put their name on a piece of paper and just take someone else's place!"

"Why didn't you tell me about this right away when you knew about it?"

Ben jumped up on Big Boy and rode hard crossing the river and out on the prairie. He had to let his roller coaster of emotions play out before he said something he would regret. He knew that Jed had done what he felt was right, but if he thought it was right, why hadn't he told him about it? It came down to one question. Did he trust Jed or not? He decided that he did and once he calmed down he was ashamed of his behavior.

When he looked around Ben realized that he was sitting on Big Boy in the tall prairie grass, not moving. Without direction, the horse had slowed and finally stopped. He was munching grass and just standing there patiently waiting for Ben to decide where he wanted to go.

Slim and Mary stayed out of the conversation. They felt they were in the way with so many emotions displayed. They asked permission to sleep in the barn and Beth made them as comfortable as she could.

Ben had returned in an apologetic mood and everyone relaxed.

After the children were asleep the five adults sat around the campfire and talked about the land that slim had chosen.

They would leave first thing in the morning for the settlement to claim that piece of land and collect their wagon that waited beside Sam and Helen's store. Several of Tom's lumberjacks had volunteered to look after all the animals and made sure the small settlement was secure while everyone else was away.

Slim and Mary went straight to the land office when they arrived at the settlement. After a few minutes of talking to the agent, Slim came out waving the paper and praising God for the best piece of land that he could ever imagine.

Slim and Mary were eager to be back on the trail to their new place. Mary held two year old Adam on her lap as they rolled along the trail beside the Silver. They kept their night camp as simple as possible and stopped only to rest when Slim knew it was necessary for his team of horses.

Mary began to feel apprehensive as they traveled farther from the settlement. She was aware of the danger in being so far from others.

Slim had described the spot to Mary in such detail that she felt like it was home before she had stepped from the wagon into the long grass.

He showed her and the children the spring and the clearing in the woods, and then explained about the way Ben, Jed and Beth had used the natural landscape to catch the wild horses in the river.

"Oh Slim, this is home!"

CHAPTER FIVE   A NEIGHBOR

That morning Jed had brought in two eggs, which when added to what they had, made enough so that they each had a thick slice of French toast and maple syrup with their morning coffee. They prayed together and asked God's blessing on Slim, Mary and their boys, as they made the trip to the settlement to claim the piece of land they had chosen. They asked that God grant them the land and they thanked Him for the time together and the new friends that they would soon have living near them.

As soon as Slim and Mary left, it was back to the self-imposed long list of things they wanted to complete before winter. Beth sat on the hill beside the house weaving a large rectangular grass rug for the living room area.

She watched Jed pulling the willow branch into an arch and holding it while Ben tacked it and then tied it with rawhide. As the day went by, the chairs were nearly completed. The last step would be done by Beth. She would sand and oil the wood, as soon as the rawhide thoroughly dried.

Next they chose three, six foot long pieces of planks for the tabletop. The boards were twelve inches wide and would make a very good tabletop. Two more would become benches. Beth would have the job of sanding and oiling them too, while the men moved on to still other projects in the coming days.

She tiptoed in to check on Johnny. He was growing fast and no longer looked tiny in his bed. His cheeks were pink from the sun. She had played out on a blanket with him while the house was being built. Heading back out, she glanced up at the antlers that Ben had carved. They now hung against the stone of the fireplace. She enjoyed looking at them.

On Sunday afternoon, Ben read from the Bible, sitting on the grass in front of the new house. As they sat and listened to Psalm 98, a Psalm of praise, several ducks flew to the lake and landed. Its surface was busy with activity, and the fullness of life. Ben continued to praise God, with Psalm 33 and then Psalm 145. Beth looked down at the beautiful baby boy in her arms and was distracted from the readings just for a moment, and then she heard Ben say, verse 4 "One generation commends your works to another; they tell of your mighty acts." NIV

"God I promise you that our son will be raised in your ways and will know of all your goodness to us. Our hearts are filled with praise and thanksgiving for the wonderful heritage you have given us." She didn't realize that she had spoken out loud until Jed said, "Amen."

Ben continued until he finished the psalm.

"It says that every creature should praise God's holy name. I wonder how the animals praise him and know him. They are all part of his creation. He loves them, too," said Beth.

"I believe they do, each in their own way," said Ben.

After nine days, Beth began to get anxious about Mary and the children. She carried Johnny as she walked over to where the men were working. Johnny loved looking at the sparkling water of the lake.

"Jed, I would like all of us to go down river to see if Slim and Mary and the boys are back and make sure everything is as planned. Would you mind Ben, if we took a couple days off to visit?" she asked. "I can bake a couple loaves of bread this afternoon and we can take them some meat, too." Ben spoke up before Jed could answer. I will stay here and care for the animals, but I think you three should go. Jed, you can use Big Boy and Ginger. It won't take you but a few minutes to get there with them. Besides they need the exercise."

"You can tell Slim and Mary that I will come down to visit sometime soon."

"Will do," said Jed. "It sounds like you two have it all figured out. Let's leave early tomorrow."

Jed prepared two bedrolls and Beth bundled up more than they would need. They left early the next morning and were soon in the Parker camp. Mary and Slim were delighted to have their first visitors.

Slim had been working hard at clearing a wide path to the spring. He had also marked an outline for their modest cabin with stones. They had spaded a small garden and Mary had planted corn, tomatoes and carrots. She had even put in six hills of potatoes. She explained that she had more to plant but they hadn't had time to get the ground ready for them yet.

They had four workhorses and Jed saw that sitting inside the wagon was a large plow. "Why are you working the land for the garden by hand with a plow and horses here?" asked Jed.

"Because Mary isn't strong enough to help lift it out of the wagon and I can't do it alone."

"Let's get it down right now," said Jed. They both lifted and pulled and managed to get it out and onto the ground.

"That's what ours looked like before the Indians burned the wagon," said Beth. "Now the metal is a different color, but Calvin Briggs put new handles on it and it still works."

"Let's go make that garden bigger," said Jed. With the horse and plow, it took very little time to finish turning the soil in an area as large as they would use the first year. Slim was grateful to Jed and Beth for coming.

"I have been wondering if I have been a stupid fool," said Slim, quietly to Jed. "I have chosen to put my house right where migrant Indians like to camp. I hope it doesn't cost us our lives."

"Slim I think that someday this whole territory will be homes of pioneers. Those of us that come first will get the best land, but we also stand the greatest risk. Teach your wife to shoot and kids to stay close and alert. Always keep your rifle loaded and handy. Don't shoot unless you are forced to. Now quit worrying and tell me all about this cabin you have planned."

Both men were smiling as they walked to the knoll where the rocks marked the outline of the house. The women were by the fire preparing a meal. Beth grinned as she saw Jed demonstrating how she had told him that the bedroom on the hut had to be bigger. He was exaggerating. Both men were laughing.

Slim and Jed walked into the woods and before long a loud crash announced the felling of a tree. Jed had wrapped a rope on the big trunk and attached it to one of the workhorses. Slim coaxed him out of the trees and up to the location. By dusk the men had six logs lying on the knoll, cleaned of their branches and ready to be used for the start of the little cabin.

"Tomorrow we should be able to do better," said Jed. "We started late today." Mary's smile showed how happy she was to see the start of the cabin.

The crash of the first tree of the morning sounded out in the early morning light. Mary had a tough time keeping her boys safe. Joshua wanted to go with the men. Adam was attracted by the sparkle of the river and tried to toddle in that direction. Mary couldn't take her eyes off him for a minute.

Finally Beth asked if Mary would be offended if she braided a harness for him to keep him safe. It took a little while to fashion it but she soon had it the right size and with ties in back where he couldn't reach them to release them. Mary watched closely as Beth braided the straps.

"If I could learn to do that, I'm sure it would be very useful," said Mary. Beth showed her again doing it slowly. Mary tried and found it quite easy.

"The nicest thing is that supplies are all over the place. I have learned to use grass, horsehair, leather or reeds, whatever is at hand," Beth instructed.

Slim had pulled their covered wagon near the trees and it was in the shade in the afternoon. With a blanket on the grass, Adam was tucked under the wagon in the cool breeze, right after lunch and soon he fell asleep. Mary had fastened the harness to the wagon wheel. She was glad to have a way to be sure that her baby was safe.

Each time Slim came out of the woods with the horse pulling a log, he would stop long enough to allow Joshua to take the reins and direct the horse to the top of the hill.

"See Johnny," Beth said, "someday you will be a big boy and work with the horses." The baby laughed and patted her cheek. She had a blanket near her in the shade and placed him on it after he had been fed. He too was soon asleep.

Joshua came to his mother, showing her what he had found in the dirt. It was an arrow point, lashed to a broken two-inch shaft. He ran up the hill shooting his pretend bow.

"It will be lonely for him here. He will miss the children he used to play with," said Mary.

"Children adapt quickly to new surroundings," said Beth. "He will find ways to amuse himself. You can teach him how to fish safely and he can pick berries. He can even help dig the mud for mortar and mix the grass in. He will like doing that. It is messy!" said Beth. They both laughed at the joke. He came back to show them a green beetle he had found.

By dark the log count was at seventeen.

"It is remarkable Slim that you two have cut so many so quickly. How many logs does it take to make a wall?" asked Mary.

"I guess that depends on how long the wall is and how long the logs are," answered Slim. "Don't worry, Mary. We will be in our cabin and cozy before winter comes. Now what have you ladies cooked for two hungry men?"

"We have venison stew," Mary answered. "Also fresh baked bread, thanks to Beth. She brought us two big loaves."

"That is great!" said Jed, as he shook the water from his hands and flipped his hair back and tied it.

Slim sat down on the grass with a file and started to sharpen the teeth of the saw they had been using.

"This was my dad's and it has seen better days. Some of the teeth aren't in line like they should be and they are all pretty worn, but I think it has one more cabin in it." Jed suddenly wanted to go home. He had an uneasy feeling, something he couldn't quite put his finger on. He knew he couldn't stay there much longer.

He had come to visit and to help them get started. He had done that and more.

"Slim I think it might be a good idea if we went hunting in the morning," Jed said. "If we are successful the women can get the meat drying while we cut a few more logs. I want to leave midafternoon." Beth was not surprised by his announcement. She could tell just by the way Jed stood that something was bothering him.

"Ben said he would come down and visit in a few days," offered Beth. "That would be mighty fine," said Slim, but his quick smile was missing.

Beth had woven two large collection baskets while she was there. She took Mary for a walk on the tree line and just inside the woods and pointed out anything she recognized. She picked the leaves of one plant for tea and another to cook as a vegetable. She pointed out maples and told her how Ben had tapped them in the fall and boiled the sap to make syrup. Inside the woods they could see hickory nut trees and raspberry bushes loaded with hard little green knobs that would develop into sweet red berries. Near the spring, fennel ferns grew in abundance. Beth told her about cooking the center tender fronds. She told Mary about gathering grain from the prairie and keeping the wild oats separate. She mentioned that she should watch for a bee tree too, so they could get some honey.

"Ben and Jed taught me most of the things I am telling you. When I joined the wagon train I didn't know how to do anything," confessed Beth.

"Mary, you have so many things here in the wild that you could survive without a garden. You will have fish and you can trap rabbits."

"Beth you make it all sound so easy. I am frightened. I have never been so far from people before. I don't know how to forage for my food like an animal!" She started to cry. Then Adam woke up and he started to cry. Joshua came running.

"What is the matter, Mom?" he asked.

"Your mother is just tired, dear. I think I am going to make her some tea. She will be fine. Maybe you can pick her a beautiful bouquet of flowers. That will make her smile." Satisfied with the reassurance he hurried off to gather the pretty blooms that dotted the prairie.

The two men were more than a little lucky with their hunt. Jed shot a large deer and as they were cleaning it a black bear had come out of the brush and Slim had taken it, too.

"That fur will be cozy this winter, he said. He isn't too old. Maybe we can eat the meat." Jed had remembered what Ben said about Big Boy being gun shy so he had taken Ginger. She sidestepped every time he brought her near the bear.

"She is afraid of it. We will have to make a travois and have her pull it out."

Slim's horse had no problem carrying the deer once they managed to load it, but she didn't want to go near the bear either.

"I have more rope and a couple of old hides at the wagon. I'll go get them." Slim hurried away leaving Jed to guard the bear. Jed worked at cutting two small trees for the poles while Slim was gone. Soon he returned and it was a simple matter to roll the bear onto the hide of the temporary travois and rig a rope harness so that Ginger could pull it the short distance, back to camp.

Mary couldn't believe her eyes when the men came into camp with a bear. Beth had already started to make drying racks and had a huge deer roast over the fire. Jed suggested that they dig a big cache and find something to secure the top before they did anything else. Slim produced a shovel and pick and they began to dig it where it would be inside the cabin when it was done. Mary and Beth both worked hard at making cord. They had already stripped the tendon from the deer and had one rack up and standing near the fire. Jed could see that Beth was feeling pressured. He knew her well enough that he could tell she would not be happy leaving until all the meat was sliced and drying.

As she worked on the cords, she suggested various things that Mary could use to line the cache so the meat would stay clean. Then she told her how Ben had plastered the grain cache.

"That was a good idea. I think I want to try that for a second cache when we get other things done," said Mary. Jed came over to the campfire and started to assemble an armload of straight branches into a rack. Slim followed his example and did the same.

The four sat in the grass slicing meat and sharing their plans for the future. Slim wanted a split rail fence along the river, a corral and a barn. He wanted to dig an irrigation system so that he could farm his acreage. Jed was dazzled by the ambitious plans. "Jed what do you plan to do?" he asked. "I would like to get a big barn up and a corral built before winter. Next summer I want to try to dig a well. That is one thing you won't need to do for a while, with that fresh spring water close by," replied Jed.

"Eventually I would like to have a herd of cattle and lots more horses," said Jed. "I would like to breed good horses and sell them." Jed stood up and took both hides to the edge of the woods and pegged them out and started to scrape. He asked Mary if she knew how to do it and she shook her head no.

"But Slim does," she said. Slim walked over and knelt beside Jed.

"This is never very much fun, is it?" he said, "but the end result is sure worth it." They worked side by side for a few minutes and then Jed got up and told Beth to gather up the things she had to take back home because it was time to leave.

Mary looked like she was going to cry again. Beth hugged her.

"We are just up the river a little way and you can come up for supper any time you like. Now don't fret. We will come back from time to time." Slim looked up at Jed and looked like he was being deserted.

"Slim it has been good working with you. You will have a nice place here, but it will take a lot of work, patience and love." He hugged Mary and shook Slim's hand and noticed that it was blistered from the saw.

"Bear grease mixed with pounded clover will help with those blisters," said Jed. "Bye now. We will see you soon." Jed turned Ginger around slowly and headed her toward home. Big Boy took his pace from Ginger and just ambled along munching now and then. He didn't try to bite Jed the way he had Ben. He was learning to trust.

"It was a nice visit, wasn't it?" said Beth with a smile.

"I'm glad they are there for you to visit," answered Jed. "You and Mary can swap recipes and baby advice. She gives me the impression that she is the one that will need a lot of advice though, about a lot of things," he said as he examined his own sore palms. "Guess I'll use some of that grease and poultice mixture when we get back if there is any left. I think that would be a good thing to keep around for small hurts."

They pulled the horses up by the corral gate and looked around for Ben. Sunshine and Rascal came bounding up to greet them. When Beth reached down to give pats and scratches, Sunshine stretched up carefully and gave Johnny a little lick on his fingers. He gurgled and laughed out loud. Rascal grabbed a corner of the blanket wrapped around Johnny and began to tug and growl. Jed quickly removed the blanket from the pup's mouth and scolded.

"You should be more like Sunshine. You ruffian! No! Stay down."

Ben laughed as he came down from the bluff.

"You sure named him correctly, Beth. I am glad to see you are back. I really missed you. So tell me all about your visit."

"Well, they have decided to put the house on that little knoll where the woods and river form a corner," said Beth. Jed told about getting the land worked up for their garden.

"We cut a few trees and got him started with that, and went hunting. I shot a deer and Slim got a black bear. He was working the hides when we left. He seems a little overwhelmed," said Jed, "but I'm sure he will be fine."

"Mary seems to have a lot to learn. Her hands are full with that two year old. Adam is on the go every minute," said Beth.

"Not bad for a three day visit. Do they have decent shelter if we get a bad storm?" asked Ben.

"I think so. They have their wagon and if it got really bad they could crawl under it instead of inside. He is a good shot," said Jed, "and I saw lots of hides they can use to rig a wind block if they wanted to."

"That's good. I want to go see how they are doing in a few days, but right now I need to let you know what has been happening here," said Ben. "We need to reinforce the barn door. The stallion came. He cracked the center board. He brought his herd right here by the barn. He has some beautiful wives and babies, more than when we first saw him. He has one that looks like she is a purebred. I think that stallion is good at stealing mares," said Ben

"We will need to be vigilant, that's all," said Jed. "What else?"

"Well, I saw several columns of smoke coming from the direction of the wagon trail. I didn't want to leave here to check it out. Did you notice it?"

"No we didn't. I don't think you could see it from Slim's place. He has so many trees around. He isn't up very far, either. I pray that it isn't another raid on a wagon train."

"I didn't get much done here, because I was up on the bluff a lot. Can you believe it, yesterday that Rascal figured out a way to get all the way up there? He followed me. I was afraid he would fall and get hurt."

"That dog is something else!" said Jed.

"Say, did Stump follow you when you left? I haven't seen him for two days!"

"That's strange. He usually comes back at night. We haven't seen him since the morning we left. He was here then," said Beth.

"I sure wish he would stay home," said Ben.

Once the horses were put in the barn and all the animals cared for, the little group walked up to Jed's house. On impulse Ben gathered a handful of stones and tossed them at the ducks. He hit a large mallard that bobbed on top of the water.

A big splash announced Stumps return as he retrieved the duck. Ben laughed and hugged the wet dog. Rascal bounded around and entered the water just far enough to get his front paws wet, and then retreated.

"I don't think he likes the water the way Stump does," said Ben.

"Well he can't be a mountain goat and a fish too," said Jed with a laugh as he opened his front door. Ben handed the duck to Beth. Sunshine hurried in and jumped up on a chair wagging her tail. The last rays of the sun touched her beautiful tri-colored coat and reflected in her coal black eyes.

Beth had worked on the curtains for the windows and had used most of her yellow calico dress length for the bedroom curtain. She put white in the kitchen window and tied them back with a grass braid. The living room curtains were white too, but she had cut a strip and dyed it dark brown creating a ruffle tie back with it. She made mats for the chairs of dark brown leather. Ben had generously given her the big bearskin from his bed and she placed it on the floor near the chairs for Johnny to play on. Her large grass mat was down nearer the kitchen area.

"He will enjoy it this winter," she had said. Their house had a welcoming homey feel when they entered.

As she strolled out to see what the men were doing, she realized that she could see the size that the barn would be. They were making it larger than Ben's. They had driven markers into the ground and dug holes and had the corner supports standing up.

A week sped by and no mention had been made of Slim or Mary. Everyone was busy with projects and plans.

Once again she began to feel concern for them. She knew that Ben and Jed worked as a team and many things they did required the strength of both men. At the evening meal she casually mentioned that she wondered how Mary and Slim were getting along. Ben said that he had been thinking about them, too.

"Tomorrow is Sunday and I think I need to rest and spend time with the Lord. I like to read the Bible alone sometimes but I really feel the blessing when we read together on Sundays. Monday morning I will head out early and go see them."

"Thanks Ben, that's a relief. I'm sure that Slim will enjoy seeing you and you will probably come back in need of another day of rest. They have so much to do," said Beth.

"Beth, you are forgetting that Ben did it all alone and he was younger than Slim. They will be fine. They are happy there. They have a beautiful piece of land, with the river and woods with the spring, its perfect and they have each other. You needn't feel sorry for them."

"I know but somehow it all seems so much harder for them. Mary is frightened. I don't think she had any real idea of what she was getting into."

On Sunday they sat on the new porch. The necessary chores were completed before a bountiful and delicious breakfast was eaten.

"It is getting easier to use the new kitchen," said Beth. "I think I finally know where I have put things." The men laughed a little, sympathizing. Ben picked up his Bible and handed it to Jed.

Jed smiled and laid it on his lap.

"I wish that I knew where in the Bible there is a blessing for a new house, or a prayer to cleanse our land after John Gray's blood has been spilled on it. I feel something strange when I walk in the area where that happened."

"Let's walk down there near my corral, and read and pray," said Ben. He led the way, carrying Johnny. They stood silently together, where it had happened.

When Ben looked up holding back his own tears, he saw that Jed and Beth were doing the same.

"He did a terrible thing, but we must forgive him," said Beth.

"Yes, you are right. John Gray, I forgive you," said Jed.

"John Gray, I forgive you," repeated Ben.

"I forgive you," said Beth, very softly. "But I still miss Bold One so much." They entered the hut and sat on the benches near the table as Jed read psalm 25.

When Jed got to; verses 11-13 NIV, "For the sake of your name, O Lord, forgive my iniquity, though it is great. Who, then, is the man that fears the Lord? He will instruct him in the way chosen for him. He will spend his days in prosperity, and his descendants will inherit the land." He paused.

"If John Gray had followed that, he would have had all he needed and would not have been carrying around a poster with a price on his head. I think I want to mark his grave with a big rock. I will chip in his name, the date he died and Psalm 25 11-13. If anyone wants to know more, they can look in the Bible. Jed had no way of knowing that by chance, he had chosen the same scripture to read that Melanie had recited when she prayed for the man's soul.

Ben left Monday morning with both horses. Beth had insisted that he take many things to help Mary. She had baked bread again and sweet rolls with bits of wild apple and cinnamon. She had used scraps of leather and stitched them together to make potholders. She had two more baskets made that she used for the baked goods and instructed Ben to leave them for Mary. She prepared the leather cooking pouch and filled it with a cooked roast. Jed shook his head in disbelief as Ben left camp on Big Boy leading Ginger with her big bundle.

"Woman, it's a good thing that you aren't a merchant," Jed said.

"Why?"

"Because I think you would give away more than you sold!"

95

"God gave us so much," replied Beth. "It is only right that we should share," she said. "Now let's get to work. We can't take the time off just because Ben is gone," she teased and handed Johnny to him. "Your son is getting heavy. Please carry him back to our house for me." They checked the garden as they passed and peeked into the den from habit. The pups bounded along behind them. Stump was nowhere in sight but they were used to him disappearing for long periods.

"I forgot to tell you with all that has been going on," said Jed, "but I have made great progress with our horses. I rode Angel for quite a while yesterday while you were working in the garden. She seemed to enjoy just getting on the prairie and stretching her legs. I put a good size bundle on surprise and he went with us. He thinks the whole thing is a lark."

"That's good Jed.

"How are you getting on with Princess?" he asked.

"Well, not too well to be honest," she said with a little frown. "We should have called her "Surprise"! She was so shy and gentle when she was little, but now she won't do anything I want. She tries to run away every time I lead her out of the gate. She throws the bundle off her back before I can get it fastened!"

"It sounds to me that she is behaving like a typical female!" He said it with a laugh. "She is old enough now to want to go to that herd she came from. Remember they are back in the area."

"Oh Jed, you are probably right. I didn't think of that!"

"I better go up on the bluff and check things out." said Jed. "If you will take Johnny the rest of the way, I'll go back and take a quick look. I think I will make sure the pond is full, too, while I'm there," said Jed. Beth suggested that she would start preparing something for them to eat.

"Sounds like a good idea to me," said Jed.

CHAPTER SIX   WHAT HAPPENED?

As Ben neared the Parker camp, he knew right away that something terrible had happened. It was too quiet. Things had been pulled from the wagon and were scattered around on the ground in disorder. He could see one of their big horses in the distance. There was no sign of the other horses or the family. He tied Big Boy and Ginger to a tree and called out several times. Ginger stomped her foot and showed that she felt distressed.

Finally from the woods came a small shaky answer from Mary as Slim came down the path from the spring. Mary followed with the children hesitantly.

"What happened here?" Ben asked. His voice was filled with concern.

"It was a really big bear!" said Joshua, sticking his head around from behind his father. "He was throwing everything!"

"Why didn't you shoot it?" Ben asked. "I was working in the woods cutting a tree down, and I left the rifle here with Mary. She was afraid to shoot in case she missed."

"I thought he was going to kill us!" said Mary.

"I think he was after your food," said Ben. "Mary, I told you that you are a better than average cook," said Slim, trying to relieve the tension.

"Well, I think you can use this," said Ben, as he pulled a rifle from the bundle and handed it to Slim. It's the rifle that was in Big Boy's saddle.

"You can't give us a rifle! You might need this yourself sometime," argued Slim.

"We each have one and an extra," said Ben. "I want you to take this one and these shells and practice with it, Mary, until you can hit a fly in flight!" They all laughed. She hugged him.

"Thank you, Ben; I know I'll feel better knowing that we both have a gun nearby. Now I guess I have my work cut out for me, cleaning up this mess." Mary started picking things up and putting them neatly back in the wagon. "I hope that big greedy fellow left us something for a meal," she said.

"Don't worry about that, Beth has packed you so much food that I think she has made Ginger permanently sway- backed!" said Ben. They all laughed as they pulled the bundle off from Ginger and Ben tied her where she could reach both water and grass.

Ben still didn't trust Big Boy not to take off, but he decided to give him a try. He pulled the saddle off him and let him loose. Both horses moved to the river for a drink and then stood in the rich tall grass side by side munching.

"See there, that's what good treatment and a beautiful lady can do," said Slim. "It is spring and he is sticking close to Ginger."

"I think you are right," said Ben.

"I'll be glad when I get a corral built," said Slim. "Our horses are scattered all over the prairie. That bear scared them away."

"How long has it been since the bear was here?" asked Ben.

"It's been a few hours. We were in the woods there hiding, thinking he might come back and I could down him. I took my gun when we hid."

"Ginger was fidgeting when I first tied her. I think she could smell that bear," suggested Ben.

Nothing was badly damaged. As they cleared up the area Mary said she had picked a bowl of strawberries and the bear had eaten every one of them.

"I sure didn't intend to pick those for a bear!" she said.

"Well, Mary, that's a good story you can tell your grandchildren someday," said Ben.

Joshua ran around shooting imaginary bears, while Mary prepared a small meal. Adam was safely fastened to the wagon wheel playing with chunks of wood and pinecones. He held a small branch that he galloped across the grass.

"He loves the horses," said Slim. "Maybe someday we will have more riding horses than just Dixie to use." Ben made a mental note to carve a horse for Adam and a toy gun for Joshua. He thought it was a little strange that the boys didn't seem to have any toys in the wagon, but he didn't say anything about it.

Slim and Ben walked up the small hill to inspect the progress that had been made on the cabin.

"It's a hard job but I can do it."

"I think you have done really well for only being here a few weeks," said Ben.

"Mary has been a good sport about living out of the wagon," said Slim, "But I would like to get the cabin done for her as soon as I can."

"How did you do the other night when that rain went through? I was thinking about you." asked Ben.

"It was uncomfortable, but we made it. I think every time we go through something new it just makes us stronger," said Mary.

"That's a good attitude Mary. What did you have planned to do today Slim, before that bear paid you a visit?"

"Just more of the same, I have been cutting logs for the house."

"Let's go see how many we can get cut before dark," said Ben. They entered the woods and disappeared.

Mary could hear the sound of the crosscut saw and smiled. They had good friends here, she thought, people willing to stop their own work to help them. She peeked at Adam and lifted him onto a blanket. He was sucking his thumb and would soon be asleep.

The Land's Heritage

After scraping the deer and bear skins they had staked out, she sat in the grass under a tree near him and picked up a mat she was weaving. It wasn't perfect, but it was better than the last two. She was so grateful to Beth for teaching her some new skills. She was learning. It pleased her. She knew that it would get easier with time and practice.

This was the third deer hide she had processed. It was going to be softer than the other two. Slim hadn't taken time to do a lot of hunting, so when he took time, he tried for the larger animals. That way they had fresh meat for a while and some to dry for winter. They had one grass-lined cache full of meat and she had surprised Slim by digging a second one while he worked in the woods. It was lined with grass and ready to be filled. She thought about the clay lining that Beth had mentioned but decided not to try it yet. Both were located so that they would be inside the house but away from the fireplace.

They had set snares by the rabbit runs down by the river and she also had a growing stack of rabbit hides that would make good winter mitts or a coat for Adam. Every day she took Adam and with Joshua along beside her they would explore a new area in the woods. She had found a pair of trees in bloom that looked like apple blossoms. She was excited to see what they would be. She discovered trillium in bloom and had transplanted some to a spot along the path to the spring so that she could enjoy them when she went to get water. The raspberry bushes were loaded with green berries and they would make wonderful preserves and fruit leather as a treat for winter. There had always been fruit leather at home for winter treats. Her mother and sisters would pick the raspberries and wash them and then press them into a smooth layer on a greased cookie sheet to dry in the oven at a low temperature. When the berries were dry and felt like leather it was cut into strips and rolled and placed in jars to keep. The best discovery yet was a patch of blackberry bushes and they too were covered with hard green berries that would be delicious when ripe.

An oven would make pies and bread possible. I wonder what it would take to make one. Maybe Ben knows how. It is worth asking, she thought.

When the sawing stopped and the men appeared, many trees lay waiting to be stripped of their branches and dragged to the cabin site. Slim smiled at Mary as she told him that she had made bean soup for supper. Both men went to the river to wash and Mary got out bowls and spoons.

As they sat eating near the camp fire, Big Boy came over and stood near Ben.

"They are used to being put in the barn about now. I guess they are wondering where they will spend the night," said Ben. Ben had tied Ginger or she would have moved closer also.

"I was hoping that our horses would come back after they calmed down," said Slim. "Maybe they will yet."

"Do you want to go look for them?" asked Ben. "If they are not back by morning, maybe I better. I don't want them joining up with some wild herd," said Slim.

"We have at least an hour of light left, let's try now," suggested Ben. "If we get them back, it will be less time away from cutting logs tomorrow."

"That's true and they could wander further away during the night. Ok I'm done eating anyway," said Slim.

"That was good soup, Mary. Thanks a lot," said Ben. He swung up on Ginger holding the simple set of reins that he had made. He held his rope in his hand. The saddle was put back on Big Boy. Slim stepped up in the stirrup and settled into the saddle just in time to hang on with all his might. Big Boy was up to his old tricks. Slim laughed as he said, "I forgot about you telling me that he does that. It must be his way of saying howdy."

Both men laughed as they rode down the edge of the trees that bordered the river. They spotted three of the four workhorses standing together in a clump of evergreens. Near them his saddle horse stood grazing. Slim slid off Big Boy and handed Ben the reins. He took the rope and walked slowly to the horses. Until he got within ten yards, then he did something that puzzled Ben as he watched. Slim sat down in the grass and started to sing a song. One by one the horses came and nudged him. Each in turn was given a scratch on the ears and a pinch of sugar from his shirt pocket as he looped the rope around their necks.

The saddle horse came up behind him and knocked his hat off. He hugged her and swung up on her bare back, leaning forward, he scratched her ears.

"Dixie and I have been together since she was a baby, sort of like you and your Ginger. I think by morning she might have brought these three back. I don't know why the other one is staying out there alone. We could see her in the distance and I called to her but she didn't come. Let's take these back and tie them to the trees and see if we can get the last one," said Slim.

It was growing dark. The moon gave enough light to barely see their way but spotting a horse might be tough. As they rode along they heard a whinny.

"I heard her over there," said Slim. He turned and rode slowly in that direction. There she stood.

The rope that Slim had used to tie her to a tree was still around her neck. The end was frayed from dragging and it had tangled in brush.

"This poor girl has been standing here all day." After scratching her ears, the rope was untangled and Slim slid up on her back. "We will follow you back Ben. She needs a little extra time with me so she knows that it's all right back at camp," said Slim. Ben led Big Boy back toward the campfire slowly, letting Ginger find her own footing in the dark. The friendship between Slim and his animals warmed Ben's heart. If I ever need someone to care for my animals, I want him, thought Ben.

The children had been bathed and they were asleep in the wagon. Mary sat beside the fire in her rocking chair, knitting.

"I thought I might have to come find you boys," she said teasingly. Slim gave her a little peck on the cheek and told her that all the horses were fine. "It will be nice to have a corral and barn someday," she said, as she poured a bit of hot coffee for Ben and Slim. "Ben you must be tired after this long day. You can put your bedroll any place you like. We usually sleep under the wagon, so we are near the boys.

"I think I'll sleep right here in the parlor," he joked. Ben settled under a tree close to his horses. He looked up at the moon remembering the last time he had slept out on the ground was after holding hands with Melanie. He was doing his best to be patient, but the time wasn't going nearly fast enough. He wanted to see her. His prayers were mixed with a feeling of longing, as he mentally listed all the things he thanked God for and all the people that he wanted God to bless. He wanted to go see Melanie, but even more, he wanted to go find Sarah. He thanked God for Big Boy, knowing that the big horse could easily carry him to search for Sarah. He fell asleep wondering if perhaps he could leave the place in Jed's hands and go look for her soon. I could go and be back before snow falls, he thought, as he drifted to sleep.

The next morning Ben and Slim worked cutting logs, cleaning the branches from them and pulling them, from the woods, until late in the afternoon. They stopped just long enough to have some food and then they worked until dark building their own version of a ramp to pull the logs up so they could peg them into place by using the horse's power to slide them up. Both men were excited to start the next morning to try their invention.

"Mary, by nightfall, you will see the first part of the walls of our cabin standing!" announced Slim.

"Which of the horses should we use?" asked Ben. "It has to be strong, smart and have patience. The logs have to go up by inches. One jerk and the whole triangle could tip over taking what we have done with it."

"Ben, I think we better use Old Bean. He is the strongest and listens well. Dixie is smarter, but she isn't as strong. I'll go hitch up Old Bean."

"We are grateful for your help Ben," said Mary.

"I'm glad to do it. I know that if I ever need help, Slim will help me. That's the way it is out here," Ben answered.

"Hey Ben, how do you want to start this? Shouldn't we put that biggest one on the very bottom?" suggested Slim.

"Makes sense to me," said Ben.

Old Bean was every bit as strong and intelligent as Slim had said. It seemed he understood after a few tries what the men were trying to do, and almost took over. All they had to do was position the logs at the bottom of the ramp and he carefully inched them up and in place and held them steady there until they had them pegged.

"That horse is a marvel!" said Ben. "He is as good as a crew of men."

"Yes and he smells better, too," said Slim with a hearty laugh.

"We don't exactly smell like French perfume right now ourselves," laughed Ben.

Slim grabbed Mary and lifted her off the ground.

"We have three logs in each of the walls of our cabin woman," he said. They were giddy with joy at seeing the progress that two days of help had made.

"You know Slim, if Mary could hold the rope on Old Bean, we could both leverage the logs to the bottom of the ramp. It would go even faster," said Ben.

"I would love to help," said Mary. "I didn't offer because I was afraid I would just be in the way."

"What would you do with the baby?" asked Slim. "He needs you, Mary. He can't be around those big logs being moved. He would get hurt," said Slim with concern.

"Let me see if I can work that out in the morning. Let me think on it," said Mary. She was grinning from ear to ear as she walked over to the fire to stir the rabbit stew, she had cooking.

"That smells like rabbit stew," said Slim.

"It is. I have another fur for the coat I want to make for Adam." Slim smiled at her and told her he was proud of how she was learning to do so many things.

In the morning she gave one of the processed rabbit furs to Adam to play with. He kept repeating the word "kitty, kitty." He sat on his blanket and played for a long time. When he grew tired of watching the work at a distance, Mary told Joshua to go tell his little brother a story and play with him.

"If you can keep him happy until noon, you will share a piece of the sugar candy as a special treat after your lunch." This kept both children busy for a while. When Adam began to whine again, they realized that it was past noon. They took a break and had a little lunch. Mary couldn't believe her eyes when she looked at the growing walls of the little cabin more than half way up.

"It doesn't seem to be going much faster, but it sure is easier on the back with two to steady the logs," said Slim. "I think we should cut more logs tomorrow. What do you think Slim?"

"I like that idea. It will give me more to work with when you leave, and it will give Old Bean a rest," replied Slim.

"He is looking a little tired," observed Mary.

"What do you think we should do this afternoon? Do you want to try one of the other horses or go hunting?" asked Ben.

"Maybe we could do both," said Slim.

"Let's try Daisy, and if she can do it, let's put the last of the cut logs into place and then go hunting." Mary got up from her rocker and went over to Old Bean. She rubbed the horse's ears and when no one was looking, she slipped him a piece of the sugar candy.

"You earned a special treat. You worked so hard," she said.

She went to the edge of the river to wet a cloth to clean Adam's face but stopped in her tracks. A huge deer was drinking from the river on the other side. She slowly moved back to the fire and told the men to get their guns.

"God has done the hunting for you. All you have to do is finish the job." Slim stood up with his rifle in his hand. He silently went down the same path that Mary had used. The deer was still there. Ben had followed him with his gun, but knew if Slim had a chance that he would only need one shot. The job was finished.

"Now how do we get him across to our side?" asked Slim.

Let's clean him over there," said Ben. They trimmed branches and lashed them together to make a raft. Ben dove in, clothes and all and took the raft across with no problem. He looked up to see his friend still standing on the bank.

"What are you waiting for?" yelled Ben.

"Can't swim," Slim answered. Slim stood there looking helpless.

"Use your horse to cross." By the time Slim got his horse and courage enough to enter the river on horseback, Ben had the deer cleaned; casings and stomach washed out, and was waiting. Slim was as white as a sheet when he finally got to the other side.

He apologized over and over. Ben reminded him of what Mary said, that new experiences just make him stronger and more capable and that he understood because he was afraid of a few things too, but said, he wasn't about to say what they were right now, and they both laughed.

Dixie pulled the deer onto the raft, and was easily able to cross and pull the raft back to their camp. Ben swam along the downstream side of it to keep it steady.

"Maybe you should save that raft. You might need it again," said Ben. Together they pulled it up the riverbank.

Ben walked over to Mary and whispered something in her ear. She nodded, then giggled and stood up. They each grabbed an arm and dragged Slim to the shallow edge of the river.

"Slim you need to learn to swim and there is no time like the present. Mary and I both know how, and if you get in trouble, we will pull you out."

"Now you can go in and do it on your own or we are going to put you in."

"Joshua, hang onto your brother so he doesn't get near the water," said Mary. We are going to give your daddy a swimming lesson." Slim hollered and bellowed

111

and squirmed as they dragged him out far enough that his feet could not touch bottom. He splashed and coughed and bobbed under but came back up like a cork.

"Go all the way across, Slim!" Ben had to shout to be heard above the racket Slim was making. Mary took a mouth full of water and started coughing, because she was laughing so hard.

Finally Ben had mercy on him and turned him back toward camp. By the time he was back where it was shallow enough to stand he had drifted down river quite a ways. Ben stayed right beside him, encouraging and urging him on. Mary got back out right beside the children. She still hadn't stopped laughing.

When Slim and Ben finally walked into camp, Slim was so tired that he flopped on the mats she had made.

"That was a darn fool thing to do. You could have drowned me!" he said.

Mary started laughing again.

"That was the most fun I have had since the wagon boss slipped on the horse plop! And this was a whole lot cleaner!" she said. Slim started with a little chuckle and then a small laugh. Before long they were all laughing hard. Mary pointed her finger at the two boys.

"You two are going to learn how to swim, too. It will be a lot safer for you with that river so close."

Ben skinned the deer and Mary pulled the hide to the edge of camp and staked it out and started scraping it like an expert. Slim pulled the drying racks from the edge of the woods where they stood out of the way when not being used. Ben was impressed by the way the couple had improved their survival skills in such a short time. Slim put their biggest kettle on the edge of the fire to hold the pieces of fat. Mary came over to the fire and slid a frying pan near the heat. She added fat and wild onions and told the men to slice the heart and liver into the pan.

"That can be our meal tonight. Once it is cut up and in there, I will let it sear. We can cover it and pull it off until we are ready to finish cooking it. I think I can finish this meat slicing now. You have helped with more than half of it. That way you can go cut more wood or whatever."

"Mary, I am amazed at all you have learned to do since you got here," said Ben.

"We all do what we have to, don't we?" She answered with a smile. She knew Ben's story and saw how he had managed. Ben, you are an inspiration.

Using Daisy made the work of positioning the logs a lot harder. She just didn't quite understand what was wanted of her until they were nearly finished.

"I think she will be able to do it easier next time," said Slim. Mary had taken the boys and a basket and gathered greens and roots after she finished slicing all the deer meat. She had pulled the pan of grease far to the side of the heat where it would slowly render.

While she washed the greens at the river, she put Joshua to work, shooing the flies away from the drying meat with a big bouquet of small leafy branches. She had put the hooves and knee joints on to simmer in a little water. Ben had told her that it would make strong glue. Things were getting done and she was learning.

CHAPTER SEVEN   A GAME AND A LESSON

The next morning they got up to see an overcast sky.

"If it starts raining, what am I going to do with all that meat?"

"Just roll it all up in its own hide and tuck it in the wagon until the rain is over," said Slim. "It's a bother, but at least I won't need to carry water to the garden today if it rains.

"Come on Slim. We can cut logs until it does come down," said Jed.

A few minutes later the men were coming out of the trees carrying the saw and hatchet as the first big drops fell. Ben tossed his saddle under the wagon, hoping that would keep it dry. Mary had put all the meat and hides in the wagon. She had put several coals and a bit of wood in one of her pans and set it under the wagon, hoping that they could keep it going. Ben noticed that there was a big pile of branches under there to help keep them dry too.

With the boys inside playing on their beds; the first few drops started to come down. Adam crawled over to the opening at the back and stuck his little palm out and giggled as the rain landed on it. Mary's rocker and the grass mats were tucked under the wagon to keep them dry. She had skillfully blocked the side of that area with an oiled hide. Mary treasured her rocking chair.

They had kept only a few of their favorite household items.

As the trail became more difficult, like many of the travelers, they had left items along the way to lighten the load. Slim had not been willing to part with his plow. The future they had planned depended on its use.

"You didn't leave much room for a man to crawl under here," said Slim, as he reached the wagon and dove under on his belly. Ben crawled in beside him, squeezing under the axle.

"Slim, reach in that saddle bag and pull out the small pouch," said Ben. He did and handed it to Ben.

"What have you got in there? It is too heavy for tobacco."

"It's a game," said Ben. "I don't chew or smoke." He spilled the five smooth stones on to the grass and showed Slim that one of the stones had a chip tapped out of it. Another had two.

"The object of the game is to pour the stones out without looking and say whether you are going to see, no chips, one chip, two chips, or all three. If you are right you get a point. You get to try until you are wrong twice in a row, then it's my turn. Ten points is one game." "It looks like fun. What should we play for?" asked Slim. "If I win you have to swim across the river and back. If you win, I'll stay one more day," promised Ben. The men could hear Mary telling a story to the boys in the wagon above them. The rain continued to fall and spatter and drip under the wagon. The men were getting wet but they didn't seem to mind. They were having a lot of fun and able to rest at the same time.

After the third game, the fire in the pan was still alive. Ben had dropped tiny branches in to feed it when needed. He had won one game, which meant when the rain stopped that Slim had to swim across the river. The next two games Slim won. Ben would be staying until Saturday.

Finally, Mary and the boys peeked under the wagon to see the men busy at the game and not even aware that the rain had stopped. They helped her get the campfire going again and the meat back on the racks, and then Ben announced that Slim was going swimming. All of them went to the river's edge to watch. He bravely walked in a few feet and then dove into the moving water.

Ben watched closely for any sign of trouble. Much to his joy and surprise, Slim made it all the way across without incident. He turned around and headed back, with stern resolve just as Ben and Mary saw the large tree swiftly approaching on the current. They hollered, but Slim couldn't move in time. The tree swept him along tangled in its branches, and then it rolled, pulling him under.

Ben dove in stroking as fast as he could to catch up with the tree that had trapped Slim and carried him down river, under the surface. Diving under the muddy water, he searched among the branches trying to find Slim. He came up for a breath and dove again. This time he felt a leg trying to kick free. Ben grabbed it and pushed up with all his strength. Slim went up to the surface as the tree rolled, dragging Ben with it. He held his breath and kicked free of the giant's arms.

When Ben bobbed to the surface this time, he could see Slim draped over the trunk of the tree, riding along with the moving water. He was alive but definitely in trouble.

A tree branch had slammed into the side of his head when it rolled. He had a big bump forming. Ben rode along moving slowly toward Slim, hoping that it wouldn't roll again. Finally he was able to grab Slim's shirt and tug him loose and away as the huge trunk and roots slid away on the current. Ben paddled and pulled Slim to the edge and up on the sandy bank. He rolled him over and pushed on his back trying to force the water out of his lungs. Slim gave a cough and then a whole series of coughs and opened his eyes breathing raggedly.

"What happened?" asked Slim.

"You were doing really well until you got tangled up with that big tree. It slammed into you pretty hard. It must have dazed you," said Ben. "I think we better head back as soon as you can walk. Mary and the boys are probably very worried by now." Ben helped him up and supported him as he coughed some more and struggled to clear his lungs of the muddy water.

When they entered camp, they found that Mary and the boys were kneeling on the mats near the fire, praying for God's help for Slim and Ben. As she saw them coming, she started to cry.

"Thank you, Lord Jesus, thank you," she said. "Oh Ben he nearly died! Slim I don't want you to swim ever again! I almost lost you today," she said. The tears slid down her face as she dabbed at his face with a cloth. The boys hugged him looking frightened.

"Don't cry Mary. I am going to be fine. That incident just taught me how important it is to be able to swim well," said Slim. "If Ben hadn't been able to, I would be gone now. Thanks to Ben I now know how important it really is for all of us to be able to swim, and thanks to his game, I have a friend to help me learn, for two more days!"

"Ben lets sharpen the saw and oil the blade and then get back to work," said Slim. Mary was still shaking and she wasn't about to brush this aside that easily.

"No you don't Slim Parker! You have a bad bump on your head and I'm going to put some bear grease with clover on it first and I'm going to make you a cup of willow bark tea and you are both having something to eat, before you go back to the woods and I won't have it any other way!" she said sternly.

"Yes, Ma'am!" said Slim with a crooked smile. He was glad to sit and rest a while. He was exhausted and he discovered that his hands were shaking. He hid it from Mary as he picked up a small piece of wood and adding it to the fire. She prepared some willow bark tea, putting the pan on to heat and then gently dabbed the promised bear grease on the growing purple bump.

The Land's Heritage

Ben hurried down along the water for a short ways and found the yellow flowers that stop infection and pulled one up. He brought it back to Mary, telling her where they were growing and what it was good for. He knew that the muddy water in Slim's lungs was as much a danger to him as the bump on the head. She listened carefully, scrubbed the root of the plant and crushing it, and added it to the brewing tea as he had instructed. Be sure to dry some of those plants. You will be glad you did if you ever need them.

She put the big frying pan on to heat and dropped some grease into it. She added four thick slices of the homemade bread that Beth had sent. She toasted both sides and smeared the top with wild strawberries and sugar. Ben had to admit that Mary made some tasty versions of old favorites. She had a pot of coffee made and he sipped a cup and watched Slim for any sign of head injury worse than the apparent bump. The children enjoyed the toast, too, and Adam finished the bowl of berries, as he struggled with a spoon and his fingers.

"I wish I had an oven, those berries would make a wonderful cake or pie." Ben sensed that Mary was not ready to let Slim go back to work yet.

"Mary it wouldn't be too hard for you and the boys to make the bricks and then all you have to do is find some big flat stones for the top and a shelf inside." Ben picked up a stick and drew a rectangle in the dirt. "You need to make a bunch of boxes this size. Then you fill them with clay mixed with strong grass stems and enough water to make a mud. When they are dry all the way through, you tap them out and make some more until you have enough bricks to build the oven. The fire goes in a small hole in the ground, with a shelf of rock up about knee high, keep going with rows of the bricks and then it tapers in to form a chimney at the back. You should leave a hole in the chimney so you can slide a thin rock in to adjust the draft, and another rock is used for the door."

"I think I can do it all except cut the smooth wood for the boxes. Ben, would you help me with that?" asked Mary.

"I could get started on making the bricks today if I had the boxes. Slim would you play with Adam for a little while so Ben and I can do this? It would be good for you to spend some time with him, anyway," said Mary. "You have been so busy lately that he hasn't had much attention from you."

"What do you think?" Ben asked, as he looked at Slim for approval.

"Sure, anything if it will get me a pie," said Slim with a slight smile. He was glad to delay going into the woods to pull on the handle of that crosscut saw. His head was pounding.

"Isn't it almost time for Adam's nap?"

"Yes it will be soon. If you lay down with him he will probably go right to sleep. Joshua can come and help us," said Mary, as she fastened Adam's harness to the wagon wheel.

Ben took his cue from Mary and they headed for the woods with a small handsaw, the hatchet, a hammer and some nails. Ben chose thick branches that were cleaned from the logs. He cut them into sections and split them with the grain. He explained that since the wood was rougher than if it was mill cut she should pack grass around the edges and then fill them. It would make it easier to remove the bricks. He made seven boxes. They put them in a row down by the end of the garden, where they would be in the bright sunshine all day.

Next he helped her mix a batch of the clay mud and showed her how to tamp it down so that there were no trapped air bubbles.

"Now, you must wait until they are dry all the way through. It will probably take several days. Once they are out of the molds, you can stack them behind the fire. The heat will make them harder and they will form a nice wind break while they are there, too."

"What do I do with them if it rains?"

"You can try to keep them dry by covering them with a greased old hide, but chances are the ones in the forms will be ruined. Once the oven is built, you can make a batch of clay and plaster it on the outside. After that dries thoroughly the rain will run off and not hurt the bricks at all," he said.

"Ben, how did you learn to do so many things? You are still so young."

"Jed showed me how to make the oven we have."

"When I get back to my place, I am going to start pulling stones from the river. I want to make a nice fireplace inside the hut for Melanie. It will be a lot safer than the way it is now. I helped to make the one that is in Jed's place. I experimented with plaster just before the boulder went through the roof and it stayed on the wall and got hard. I think I want to do that to the walls of the main room. It will be a lot brighter in there and cleaner, too."

They walked over to the campfire and sat down quietly on the mats. Mary poured each of them a cup of coffee. She handed Joshua a basket and told him he could look for more berries in the patch, but not to go any farther than the spring. He hurried away delighted to be trusted, to be off on his own.

Adam woke and Mary quickly scooped him up from the blanket so that he wouldn't wake Slim.

"Ben that is something we could do that would help a lot when the time comes to use them."

"What?"

"Pull some rocks out of the river for our fireplace and chimney."

"Hey that's a great idea. I'll go down and turn the raft into a skid. Ginger will pull that easily." Ben fastened more big branches together making a large platform. He bound an old greased hide to the bottom so that it would slide easily. They had to go up stream a little ways before they could find a spot that had ideal rocks and a clear stretch for the skid to be pulled. Still

123

Slim slept. Ben was getting worried, but he didn't want to say so to Mary. They worked as a team, picking out smooth rocks of different sizes and colors and piled them on the skid.

Ginger walked to the cabin site as if there was nothing on the skid.

"This sure is a good horse, and more intelligent than a lot of them too," said Mary. After two more loads, Slim finally came walking over to see what they were doing as they took the last few rocks from the skid. Ben was relieved to see that he was awake and looked refreshed.

"How do you feel?" asked Mary.

"I feel myself again. I had a terrible headache earlier but it is gone now," said Slim

"I'm so glad that you are all right after that ordeal. You needed that rest. You have been working too hard," said Mary.

Adam sat in the shade tethered to a nearby tree with his harness on, playing with his rabbit fur and some pretty stones and a tin cup that he was banging with a spoon.

"Where is Joshua?" asked Slim. "He went with a basket to pick berries by the spring. He has been gone quite a while." A look of new concern swept over Mary's features as she headed for the path to the spring.

She found him sitting on the path playing with a baby raccoon.

"Isn't he the cutest thing you ever saw Mom? Can I keep him?" he asked. "Can I?"

"He is very cute. Look at his toes. They look like fingers," she responded. "His mother is probably looking for him right now. Where did you find him?" she asked.

"He was over there in the hole in that tree. I was picking the berries and he peeked at me."

"We can't take him from his mother Joshua, but if you put him back in the tree, we could come and visit him when we get water. We can't take care of him the way that she can." said Mary. "If we leave him here, he can be our friend."

"Can I take him to show Adam before I put him back?"

"Yes, but just for a little while." Joshua ran down the path, holding the baby raccoon against his chest.

"Adam, Adam," he shouted, "look what I've got!" "Kitty," said Adam reaching for the raccoon.

"No, you can't take it. You might hurt it. You can just touch it. Joshua gently aided his brother in stroking the little animal's fur. "I have to take it back to its mother."

"I want kitty!" whined Adam.

"No Adam, you can't have it," said Mary. "Take the baby back to the tree Joshua and bring your basket back," she said firmly. Adam continued to wail.

125

Joshua headed back down the path into the woods.

"You shouldn't let him wander in the woods alone. Have you forgotten that bear already?" growled Slim.

"No I haven't forgotten it, but we were busy and he is getting big enough to be trusted a little now and then. He never has gone farther than I say he can." Slim sounded grouchy but he didn't feel that way. That was when they realized that he was hoarse and he admitted that he had a sore throat.

Mary gave Slim some honey in the last cup of tea she had made for him earlier. He sipped it and thanked her. She started a new batch.

"It must be caused by the sand in the river water," he said. "I don't mean to sound so grouchy."

"Ben you have already done a lot today including save my life, but do you have strength enough left to cut a few trees while the day cools off? I feel like I could do my part now. I don't think I could have earlier," said Slim. "If you are sure you want to try, I am more than willing to help you," said Ben.

Mary unhooked Ginger from the skid and scratched her ears.

"You are a good horse, and a good helper," she said affectionately. She led her down to the river where the other horses were enjoying the green grass.

Adam was on the blanket whining. He raised his hand toward the woods.

"I want kitty." That reminded her that Joshua had not returned from taking the baby raccoon back. She checked to be sure that Adam was securely fastened to the tree and then hurried down the path, calling Joshua's name. He met her half way to the spring. His small basket was more than half full of berries.

"Did you put the baby back where the mother could find it?" asked Mary.

"Yes Mom. She came right away and chattered at me. She didn't like me touching her baby. She sounded cross," said Joshua.

"She was afraid that you had hurt the little fellow. You found more berries! That was a lot of work picking all those. Thank you, Joshua. We can have them as a treat at our evening meal."

A loud crash announced another tree down for the cabin. She looked around the camp and decided that she should spend more time scraping the hides. She worked them faithfully for over an hour until her back was hot from the sun and sore from the work. She looked at her littlest son tethered to the tree and felt sorry for him.

"Would you boys like to go for a walk on the prairie? We can all carry a basket and see what we can find." She had made a basket for each of the boys. She poured the berries into a bowl, and rinsed out Joshua's basket. There I think we are ready. She started to leave camp but turned back and picked up the gun that Ben had brought. Guess I better get used to carrying this thing, she thought.

The dandelion leaves were getting bitter now, but she could use them if she picked just the newest leaves. Then she remembered that someone on the wagon train said they had used the dandelion blossoms for making wine. Well if they can make wine, I can make vinegar she thought. She started picking the flowers. Even Adam plucked a few and put them in his basket.

As they wandered along, Joshua found a nest of four ptarmigan eggs. He carefully put them in his basket snuggled among the yellow flowers.

His next find was his favorite. The newly shed skin of a snake lay against some rocks. He immediately handed her his basket.

"I want to take this!" he said. "Let's go back now. I want to show Dad and Ben." They had walked farther than she thought. When she glanced back in the direction of the camp she was amazed. Just then Adam stubbed a toe and fell down crying. She tried to soothe him but he wanted to be picked up.

"How am I supposed to carry a heavy gun, three baskets, and a two year old?" she asked the prairie. Somehow, she managed. After a minute of riding on her hip and holding on to his basket, Adam wanted to get back down. Joshua ran far ahead of her. When she yelled for him to wait he kept going.

"He can't hear me. He is too far!" she murmured.

Just before he disappeared into the woods she heard another crash.

"Thank you, Jesus. He didn't have time to get back in the woods where they dropped the tree."

Mary led Adam and carried the gun as she followed her son's route into the trees. She could hear his excited voice telling the men all about that big snake! She was angry with him for disobeying her, but didn't want to steal his joy of the moment. After talking to Slim and Ben, she told Joshua to come with her back to camp. She lifted Adam into the covered wagon and gave him a drink of water and a piece of jerky to chew on.

"Joshua, I need to talk to you," she said, as they stood near the wagon.

"You did something very, very wrong! Do you know what it was?" She waited giving him time to think about it. He nodded his head.

"Tell me out loud. What did you do wrong Joshua?"

"I went in the woods where they are cutting the big trees," he replied hesitantly.

"Do you remember why it is wrong?"

"Yes, Dad said that the tree might fall on me and kill me."

"What do you think we should do, so you won't make that mistake again?"

"Punish me?"

"Yes, I must punish you."

129

"What are you going to do?" he said in a concerned voice.

"I am not sure yet, but while I think about it, you are to sit in the wagon with Adam and fold your hands in your lap and not touch anything. Do you understand?"

"Yes Mama." A tear slid down his cheek as he started up into the wagon.

"Give me the snake's skin," she said. "I will put it under your mat so that it doesn't break apart or blow away." He obediently handed it to her.

Mary secured Adam to the tree again the next afternoon. She had discussed it with Slim and it had been decided that as punishment for his misdeed, Joshua had to take a nap when Adam did.

"But Mama, I'm too big for naps!" he objected. She knew that he would sleep. They had all been doing so much that a little extra rest would be good for him.

Once the boys lay safely asleep under the tree, Mary hitched Dixie to the skid and was able to bring another load of rocks from the riverbank. She was unloading it when the men came out of the woods.

"Can you believe that woman?" asked Slim. "She is the hardest working woman in the territory!"

"Mary I will unhook Dixie for you and unload the rest of the rocks. Go take a break while the boys are resting," said Slim. She was pleased that they appreciated her efforts. While she was working she had gotten an idea. If I pull all the rest of the rocks from that same area, I will have a clean, gravel lined bathing hole. I could even put a couple branches across the side where it starts to get deeper.

"What are you looking at?" asked Slim. She was standing near the river with her hands on her hips, imagining it completed.

"I'm just looking at the water." This was something that she could do without asking Slim to help. She wanted to surprise him. When she was finished with hauling rocks the skid would be a good thing to sit on to dry off, after a bath. She would just turn it over and fasten on a new hide and rub in plenty of grease to preserve it.

Mary had prepared a stew from some of the deer meat. She served it with the last of the bread. It was dry, but they poured the broth over it and the meal was delicious.

By the time that Ben prepared to leave on Saturday afternoon, the first set of bricks had been turned out onto the prairie sod and a second set was in the molds. She was so glad that she had asked Ben how to do it.

When he lifted the saddle up to put it on Big Boy he saw that it had been oiled and rubbed to a soft shine.

"Thank you Mary, for your thoughtfulness," he said. The whole family gave him many hugs. He truly had learned to love this little family. He held their hands for a moment and prayed God's blessings on them and on their efforts to create a home here. He thanked God for healing Slim of any injury from his swimming accident.

As he headed Big Boy toward home, Ginger walked beside him untethered. A simple command, of "let's go Ginger," was all that was needed.

CHAPTER EIGHT   THE CHALLENGE

Ben rode along on Big Boy, not thinking of anything in particular. He was reviewing the work they had accomplished, until Melanie's beautiful face and hair danced before him. He felt like turning Big Boy around and heading for the settlement. Fall seemed such a long way off. Ginger's whinny surprised him. Big Boy stopped and turned toward the open prairie.

There, not fifty yards away stood the stallion in front of his herd. In a heartbeat Ben knew that he wouldn't be able to keep Ginger away from him. She wasn't tied to Big Boy. She didn't even have her halter on that he could grab. Suddenly Big Boy reared up on his hind legs, unseating Ben. He considered Ginger his. He wasn't going to give her up without a fight. Ben grabbed the strap on the saddle and released the buckle of the cinch with a jerk. The saddle fell to the ground. Ben managed to steady the big horse long enough to remove the bridle and reins.

"There, at least you aren't at a disadvantage. Ginger belongs to us, Big Boy. Go protect her."

The stallion reared and screamed, pawing the air! Ben had to admit to himself that the raw untamed power was frightening. Big Boy met the challenge with equal might. He reared, bringing his front hooves down against the head and neck of the stallion, biting, and whirling, and kicking with his hind legs. The stallion brought his hooves down again and again, trying to land a critical blow. It was apparent that this was not the first

133

time that Big Boy or the stallion had accepted a challenge. His unyielding battle stance was awesome. The stallion backed up and stood a short distance away. Big Boy took a step toward him and then another. The stallion backed up again. Big Boy stomped the ground throwing his head up and down. Once again he reared on his massive hind legs. This time the stallion did not meet the challenge. He turned and fled across the prairie taking most of his herd with him.

Ben was astounded to see that Ginger stood beside two other females. One was the thoroughbred that he thought so magnificent. Now what am I supposed to do? Ben thought. One false move from me and he will take off and the three females will go with him. Then he remembered what Slim had done. He didn't have sugar, but he did have a few crackers that Mary had given him to nibble on the way home.

He sat down next to his saddle holding his rope and slowly pulled out the crackers. He started to sing a soft song and was glad when Ginger finally came over to him. He scratched her ears and slipped a loop onto her neck and gave her a cracker. He spoke softly to Big Boy, knowing that the adrenaline was still pumping through the big horse's veins at top speed. He held out a cracker and continued to drone his song. Big Boy came and took the cracker, but backed away when he saw the rope lifted toward him.

Ben decided to try a different tactic. He put the saddle onto Ginger. It was made for a larger horse, but it would stay on enough for her to carry it. He slipped the bridal on that he had made for her and slowly started to walk toward home. Big Boy followed. Soon he was walking beside Ben nudging his hand for another cracker. The other two horses followed at a distance. Ben knew that the thoroughbred had to be used to people. He stopped and held a cracker out.

"Come here pretty girl. Look at you. You are beautiful," Ben spoke in his softest voice. She took a step closer and then another. She nibbled and nudged his hand wanting more. He scratched her ears and patted her. It seemed that her body relaxed when he slipped the rope gently around her neck and fastened it to the saddle horn. She looked at it as security rather than a confinement.

One more to go he thought. I am sure glad that Mary gave me the crackers. He stopped again and this time held the cracker out to the small, brown filly that followed at the farthest distance.

"Come on little girl. It's your turn. This cracker is for you. Come on sweet girl. Don't be afraid, the others aren't afraid of me. I won't hurt you, not ever." She took one step closer.

"That's the way. You want this treat. You know you do. Come on, sweet girl." He bent down slowly and put half a cracker on the grass. She waited until he moved away and then she sniffed at it and ate it. He held out his last one hopefully. She came ever so slowly, watching his face and eyes for any sign of danger. He didn't dare to even blink as she took the cracker from his outstretched palm. He felt in his pockets hoping to find even a small piece. He was delighted when he found a generous lump of Mary's sugar candy. She must have slipped it in there when she hugged me. Bless you Mary, he thought. He broke the candy into several small pieces. She stomped nervously but was enjoying this interaction. He put one piece in his palm and held it out. He had the loop ready in his other hand.

When she took the candy the sweet new taste distracted her from the sensation of the rope being slipped onto her neck. Ben was able to fasten it without having to pull her closer.

Once it was tied to the saddle he gave her another nibble and started to walk away with Ginger. The rope tugged at her neck for the first time. She reared and jerked trying to get free. Ben wrapped the rope several loops around the saddle horn bringing her closer to Ginger. Much to Ben's surprise, Big Boy came up beside her so closely that he and Ginger had her securely sandwiched between them. She calmed down and walked along at the pace Ben set. The thoroughbred walked on the other side of Ginger. Ben gave Big Boy the last piece of candy as his reward.

"That was exciting, Big Boy. You are good at staking a claim and defending what you think is yours!"

Crossing the river was a bit difficult as each horse tried to cross independently. They all made it without getting hurt and he still had all of them.

Ben glanced at the biggest oak where his parents were buried, as he crossed. He softly told his father that he had found a horse as beautiful as Dart Away.

He went straight to the corral and opened the gate. He put the thoroughbred in first and then led Ginger in with the other one still attached to the saddle horn. Big Boy followed Ginger showing that was what he had intended the whole time. Ben pulled the gate shut before releasing the rope from them. He removed the saddle and bridal from Ginger and stood there amazed at what had just happened. Big Boy went about nudging and nibbling the necks of each, being very possessive, and including Angel in his little harem.

"I guess no one can say they aren't yours Big Boy," said Ben.

*****

Days earlier as Ben left, Jed climbed the bluff and looked across the prairie up river to see the stallion and his herd in the distance grazing. He was right. Princess was reacting to their presence. All the horses would be harder to handle as long as they were close. What a beautiful sight they are, thought Jed, as he climbed down and headed for his house. He had spotted a beautiful white foal with a cream colored mare. He wanted Beth to see them.

The pond was low. He filled it and watched Rusty enjoy his usual stomp in the water. Ben had not had time to work much with the twins, but they were big enough.

"We need to start holding school around here, Rusty." The horse immediately raised his head and looked at Jed, recognizing his name. He walked to the fence where Jed stood.

"Would you like some scratches on those ears?" he asked as he reached through the fence and scratched and patted. Missy followed him.

"Missy come here girl. You can have a scratch too." She didn't come close enough for Jed to reach her.

Jed whistled as he went up the path to the new house. He was happy inside. It just had to come out. He realized how blessed he was.

Beth sat on a blanket on the grass beside their house. She had made lunch for them and brought it outside.

"It is so lovely out here I thought that we should eat on a blanket and let Johnny get a little sun before his nap." He picked up his son and tossed him above his head. Johnny laughed out loud.

"You liked that, didn't you? Would you like to fly like the birds?" he asked as he tossed him up again.

"Jed, would you please play with him on the blanket? That is dangerous. You could drop him!"

"Ok little mother. We will stop flying for today." He rolled Johnny on to his back and tickled his tummy. "What's for lunch?" he asked, as he settled down. "I could see an unusually pretty pair of horses in that herd today. The herd is close enough to see each one. There is a cream colored mare with a pure white foal!"

"Maybe I'll climb up and take a look later. The white ones are probably related to Buddy," said Beth.

Later Jed climbed the bluff again. The horses were restless in the corral and he really wanted to work with them, but didn't want to have a problem with the wild herd. He looked up and down as far as he could see. Good they have moved, he thought. As he turned around to climb down he saw Rascal making his way up. You poor fellow as soon as you get up here, I will be heading back down. Jed sat down for a minute and scratched the ruffian's ears giving the dog time to catch his breath from the climb. I wonder where Stump is. I haven't seen him around again. Maybe he followed Ben.

"I am going to take Angel and Surprise out for a run. Rascal you can come if you want to." He put the weighted bundle on Surprise and led him out of the corral.

"You are next, Angel." The saddle that he had made was unlike any other. It was a simple leather pad with a strap that went around her middle. The stirrups were just loops. The bottom of the loop had been hardened to a useful shape, by wetting it, and then leaving it to dry with a thick branch tucked through. He used the bridle he had made from the fittings he had purchased from Matthew Morgan. He had sewn a loop to the back of the saddle so that he could lead a second horse conveniently. He attached Surprise's lead rope to it and swung up on Angel. She blew a greeting.

"Let's go".

139

"I want all of you to be comfortable with water crossings so let's take our run on the other side," He spoke to her as if he were talking to a person. They slogged through the water and Angel crossed the deeper water as if she had done it every day, but Surprise objected and jerked on his line trying to turn back. Jed spoke to him reassuringly, but gave him no chance to do anything other than cross at his mother's pace.

Once on the prairie they galloped along, traveling parallel to the trees. He turned back and walked the distance to the largest oak. They stopped and he tied Angel there in the shade.

"Young man, it is your turn to carry something besides a bundle." Surprise had no problem with Jed removing the bundle and replacing it with the saddle, but he was sure he didn't want this heavier man on his back. He reared up and came down bending forward almost to the ground, dumping Jed onto the carpet of leaves.

"Well, that wasn't very nice of you, after all the grain I have carried to you. Now let's try that again." Jed got on again and before long he once again found himself looking up at the horse.

"Now stop that!" He said. The third time he got on, Surprise stood still with his ears pressed back. He was on the verge of rearing again, but decided to race away instead.

Jed had the fastest ride he could ever have imagined! He didn't try to rein him in at all. Staying on his back at that speed was a thrill. Teaching him to respond to the commands of the bridle and his knees would come in time. Surprise ran until he grew tired. Finally he started to circle back to the river and the place where his mother waited for him. He trotted up to her and Jed quickly slid off.

Surprise's sides were heaving. He had built lather on his beautiful coat. Jed tied him beside Angel and gathered a big handful of dry grass. He dipped it in the river and began to rub the horses down with it. He changed the grass over and over again, working until Surprise was cooled down and dry, and both horses were clean and shining. He let them drink then, and stand in the tall green grass. I guess you are both cool enough now to go back across. He slid back up on Angel and led Surprise behind them.

Before he had left with Angel and Surprise, Jed had filled the pond. When he returned, a very muddy Rusty stood near the gate.

"You are a mess! Why do you always stomp in the drinking pond? Your pals in there probably get tired of drinking muddy water. I'll bet you would like crossing the river. When we get Ginger back here, she will show you how it is done." He went in the corral and rubbed the mud off of Rusty's legs with dry grass. Missy came over and wanted equal attention.

"I think you two should be carrying a bundle for a while today." He rigged up a couple and tied them on. They spent the next few minutes trying to pull them off themselves and each other.

"You can play with the bundles any way you want. Just get used to the weight on your back. I will be back in a little while to take them off," he said affectionately as he closed the gate behind him.

He led Princess into the barn and put her in the biggest stall and secured it with boards across the opening. She was still acting nervous. He gave her a rub down and fresh water and a bundle of grass.

When he came out, Buddy stood with his head hanging over the corral gate. It seemed he was indicating that he knew that he was the only horse that hadn't gotten any attention. Jed walked over and slipped the bridle on him. Buddy didn't know what to do with the bit. Jed pressed it into position and buckled it on. Next he strapped the saddle on.

"Well I'm not sure just how far Ben has gotten with you, Buddy. Let's go for a little walk." Jed scratched the horse's neck and ears and talked to him leaning on the saddle. Slowly he slid up and on. Jed was surprised at how still Buddy stood. His ears were erect and he didn't try to buck him off. "Buddy," he said, "will you take me for a little walk?" Buddy just stood there. He didn't have any idea what Jed wanted.

Ben had put a heavy bundle on his back many times, but he had never required him to run or walk along with it. Jed leaned forward, and tried to encourage him to move. Nothing happened. Jed touched his heals to Buddy's sides.

"Ok let's go." Nothing happened. Buddy was now holding his ears back and getting very unhappy. He had

142

expected Jed to lean forward and hug him and scratch his ears and talk to him the way Ben had. Buddy decided he had put up with enough of this game and reared up and dumped Jed on the hard ground near the corral gate. It happened so suddenly that it caught Jed off guard.

"Stop that Buddy. That hurt!"

He brought Angel back out and put the saddle on her and the bridle, too. Buddy was tied to the loop of the saddle. He walked Angel and then trotted around the area with Buddy following.

"See Buddy, this is how it is done". He patted both horses and put them back in the corral, returning the saddle and bridle to the barn. He tossed huge bundles of grass over the fence to be sure they had more than enough.

Later Jed worked, using Angel to drag more of the logs they had cut, to the spot where the barn would be built. He piled all the left over lumber from the house into the wagon and she pulled it easily, to the area of the new barn. Jed was aware of the good horse he had. Someone must be missing her. I will put a notice in the store when I go to the settlement.

Mid-week, they got a nice early morning rain. Jed had spent long hours weeding the garden and spaded a small garden in front of the house for flowers. The marigolds and poppies had sprouted and he was able to transplant a few. Beth was delighted.

"That vegetable garden is almost too big for a guy to weed without getting discouraged! I think you gals got a little overly enthusiastic!" he said.

"Some of the apple seeds have sprouted and we have seven skinny little fingerlings. When those get bigger we should move them. Let's put one on each side of the front yard. They would be beautiful in the spring when they are in bloom and all summer we can watch the fruit grow," said Jed. Beth thought it was a wonderful idea.

The next day Jed spent making a pair of triangles that were designed so that he could raise or lower the apex. They were fastened together at the bottom with a skid type platform. It was his idea to place a log on the two triangles at the bottom and have Angel pull it up and into place as the wall of the barn grew higher. He used her to pull the logs into position for the entire row around the outline. The second row would tell if his invention would work. Beth watched him from the blanket on the grass, as the first log of the second row was put in place.

"You are a genius! That worked well," said Beth. "I think that would be a breeze for Big Boy if he is willing. He is so strong. That is a good invention."

"Thanks. I was afraid that it might not work. Angel tries hard but she isn't a work horse. It would go better with Big Boy. I wish Ben were here to see it. If he isn't here by tomorrow night I am going to ride over there the next morning to make sure there isn't a problem. He has been gone a week. I would come back the same day. Would you mind if I did?" he asked.

"No, of course not," she replied.

"Ben said he was going to stay a couple of days. But this is Saturday and he left Monday morning," said Jed.

Beth tucked Johnny in for a nap and decided she would climb up to the top of the bluff to have a look. She could see the herd. When she got down, she told Jed that the horses were not far down river. I could see the white ones you mentioned. They look beautiful in the sun," she said. "That white foal looks like it was born recently. It is the size that Surprise was when I first saw him.

"We have enough to do right now without dealing with a visit from him," replied Jed. "I hope he stays away from here. I was out working with the horses earlier and couldn't see him. They must have been in the trees up river. I am glad I didn't run into them with one of our young ones. That could have been bad."

While Johnny slept, Beth worked sewing baby clothes out of white cotton flannel. Jed was busy working on the barn. She was nearly certain that she was expecting another baby. Something in her heart told her that another child was on the way. She smiled and listened to be sure that Johnny was still asleep.

She could hear the cackle of the chickens drifting across the lake. I would like to have Jed move them closer after the barn is done. Somewhere partly open to the sun so the rooster can crow on time, she thought.

After Johnny wakes up, I'll take him to see them and check their water. I should check the snares, too. I forgot all about them. She thought it might be a good idea to make some snares closer, on the edge of the lake. There are lots of rabbit runs. I will mention that to Jed.

When Johnny woke up it was midafternoon. She gave him a bath and took him to see his daddy. Jed walked around inside the outline of the barn with the baby riding on his shoulders, while he explained to him, where everything was going to be located. Johnny couldn't understand what his daddy was talking about yet, but he loved the attention. Jed handed Johnny back to Beth and said he wanted to get a little more done before he quit for the day.

CHAPTER NINE   MY GIRL

Beth carried her rifle, a basket and Johnny as she headed down the path toward the hut. Ben met her at the clump of pines near the wolf den. His face was flush with excitement. He grabbed Johnny from her arms and rushed back the way she had come.

"Come on Beth, I have to show this to both of you at the same time! Jed, hey Jed, Come here!" He shouted. Johnny was happy to see his Uncle Ben and cooed contentedly reaching for his face with a little gurgle sound. Even in his excitement Ben couldn't help but bend to the baby and nuzzle him with his hair tickling his tummy. Johnny laughed and grabbed both hands full of hair. Jed looked up and smiled.

"Thank God you are alright. What are you yelling about? Can't you just get home and say Hi, I'm back?" said Jed with a chuckle.

"No, I can't!" said Ben. "Come on, come to the corral and see what I brought back with me." Ben hurried the little group down the path around the lake to the corral.

Jed stopped dead in his tracks. He thought his heart would stop when he spotted the beautiful thoroughbred mare in the corral.

"She is magnificent! Where did you get that horse?"

"I didn't, Big Boy did. The stallion tried to take Ginger on our way back. He challenged Big Boy for her, and Big Boy won. When the stallion took off, Big Boy still had Ginger and two others decided to stay with him, the thoroughbred and the little brown one over in the corner near Missy."

"This is fantastic! After he got done fighting the stallion, how on earth did you get him back?"

"I didn't do that either. Ginger did. I put a rope on her and the thoroughbred was easy to get a rope on. She is used to being around people. Big Boy was still very excited. Finally when I managed to get a loop over the little lady's neck and they started to walk with me, he decided he was coming, too. He followed all the way here and walked right in the corral with them."

"Can you imagine the kind of foal she will have?" said Beth. "She looks like she has about a month to go, before we find out."

"I can't see any brand on her," said Jed. "She can't have been in the wild very long, her coat is in good shape and she still has all her shoes."

"Someone is probably pretty unhappy about losing a beauty like her," said Ben.

"You know we should brand our horses," said Jed. "We couldn't prove they are ours if that stallion or anyone else steals them."

Now that she was in their corral, he was feeling possessive and didn't want anyone to be able to take her from them. Ben had watched the process of branding and had strong feelings against it.

"I don't want to do that. Maybe we can figure out another way to mark them as ours. Let's think about it." Jed coaxed the beautiful thoroughbred to the fence and stroked her.

"She is just what we needed to start a good blood line." He was grinning and knew it was best to let the horses relax in their new surroundings but he longed to go in the corral and make friends with her.

"It's my turn now to show you what I have been doing while you were gone." Jed pointed in the direction where he had been working. They walked down the path again and Ben stopped to gaze at the beautiful clean rows of growing plants in the garden.

"I can certainly appreciate what someone did here. This garden looks good and things are doing well. Thanks guys."

"I didn't even help," said Beth. "Jed did it all."

"Well he is my hero!" laughed Ben. "It must have taken hours!"

As they walked nearer, Jed laughed and pointed at the contraption he had built to help lever the logs into place for the barn walls.

"Take a look at this and tell me what you think of it."

"Hey it looks like the top height can be easily changed by moving the bar up a notch as you go along. That's great."

"We made a ramp to use at Slim's, but each time we wanted it a row higher we had to add to the bottom support and extend the length of the ramp. This is much better," said Ben.

"You should see my Angel pull the logs up that little ramp. She is a real gem.

The men talked about leverage and supports.

"Enough of that talk. Please save that for later," laughed Beth. "Tell me about Mary and the boys and the cabin. Start at the beginning and tell me what you did every day you were there."

*****

The answer to Jed's question of where the thoroughbred came from was not that far away. The army had marched down the Silver the week after the people returned to the settlement. They had started to build the fort on the same side as the settlement. It was impressive when you saw it on the Silver River and not far away, at a spot just before the four fingers developed. Several wagons filled with supplies followed the soldiers to their location. The company officers rode horses of the finest quality, while lower ranked men rode on lesser bred but sturdy mounts.

They had lost many horses during their nights when they bedded down with their horses tied to trump lines. The Indians moved silently in the dark. They stole some and chased off more. Major Connors was sad when he lost his favorite mare. She had been bred to a dark brown thoroughbred, called Lightning, the fastest horse in the territory, just before his orders came to build this Fort. She had not been required to carry a person on her back during their move but walked along at a leisurely pace beside, or behind the lead supply wagon. She was carefully tended, loved and his personal property.

The Major had seen the herds of wild horses roaming the prairies and hoped that she was with one of them. He would prefer that to having her ridden. She would foal in a few weeks. He planned to go look for her as soon as the fort was under way and all the supplies secured. He had planned to ride the area surrounding the fort anyway, to familiarize himself with the area. Now with My Girl missing, he wanted to do it sooner. He hoped to find her before she had her foal.

The scouting party had seen a herd of wild horses on the prairie near the wagon trail, two days earlier. The Major was overly optimistic. He was sure that all he would need to do, when he saw her, was to call her name and she would come to him. He had never experienced the wrath of a possessive, wild stallion guarding his mares.

When they spotted the herd after several days of searching, My Girl was not with them.

"I will find her if it takes me a year!" He was furious and disappointed. He couldn't stand the thought of anyone else riding her, especially now or possibly misusing or abusing her.

The next day the Major sent out another scouting party. They had been ordered to map the area and find

My Girl. The soldiers wandered the area glad to get out of the hard work of building the fort. They headed north up the Silver River discovering the mud flats, small lakes farther north, deep forest, animal trails and high bluffs, recording it all on a rough hand drawn map.

One morning after several weeks of riding the territory, they saw columns of smoke rising in the distance. Heading east, cutting through a forest of pines, hickory, oak and maple, they drew near the break in the trees, to see prairie grass stretching to a shimmering small lake, and an Indian camp on the other side. To their right they could see huge gray boulders higher than a man on a horse by ten or more feet. From their location it appeared that the boulders were a natural maze without a route through them. Sergeant Allen raised his telescope peering in the distance.

More than one hundred horses grazed near the lake and were being watched by a single man playing a flute. Some of the horses were big muscled work horses. It was easy to guess that they had been taken from the wagon trains. Most of the others looked like sound riding horses.

They dismounted and waited the long hours until nearly dark to circle the camp.

"The information of how big this tribe really is will be valuable to Major Connors," said Sergeant Allen. They could occasionally hear a few notes of the flute music drifting over the distance. Very cautiously they counted the number of tents.

152

"I don't see the Major's horse. Do you?" whispered one of the men.

"No, but be quiet! Sounds will travel among these trees and across water." Once they were deeper in the woods, the Sergeant commented.

"We will look at the horses again in the morning to make sure that My Girl isn't there. I saw several horses staked behind their tents. We should go around there and check them carefully. A horse as beautiful as the Major's will get special treatment, if they have any brains at all."

At first light, he sent two men to circle around the camp and check the horses tied close to the tents.

The soldiers had seen Dart Away in the herd, but now he was tied to the back of one of the biggest tents.

"Sure wish I could get close enough to take that one back to Connors. He is a beauty."

"Why don't you try it?"

"The only thing that would get taken is my scalp! That's why!"

When they returned they said that they were sure that one of the females they had seen was white.

"She's young, with dark hair but her skin doesn't match the rest of them and she is skinny and tall."

"That's interesting. I don't remember any recent reports of a missing woman, but we should check when we get back."

"We saw a field of corn growing on the other side of the camp. It looks like they plan to be here a while."

"Let's move out. I don't want to be discovered." They rode slowly through the trees heading back in the direction of the wagon trail.

"I hope you plan on getting us new uniforms. Look at these pants. All that crawling, you had us doing has scrubbed the knees nearly through, and look at the toes of my boots! No amount of polish is going to fix that!"

"Keep quiet!"

"We better get back and tell the Major about this."

"He is not going to be happy. Not only did we find Indians, but we didn't find My Girl."

*****

"After you eat, I have to show you something," Beth said. Jed and Ben were quiet as they nibbled at their lunch. They were starting the roof and putting the extremely heavy beams up to support it.

"I Thank God, for Big Boy's strength, said Beth. I don't think the others could do it even if you hooked two of them together. You both look so tired. You need to rest. You have been working very hard. You have made great headway on the barn. Can't you take a break this afternoon?" Jed shook his head no and started to walk back to the barn.

"Jed wait, I need to show you something."

"Sorry honey, I forgot. Where is it?"

"It's in the corral."

"What did you do, catch some more wild horses?" laughed Ben.

"No, she replied with a serious tone. You'll see." She hurried ahead of them.

"Do you think it is ok if I leave Johnny in his bed alone for a few minutes?"

"It should be safe. He can't get out of that crib yet. The window is latched and his door is shut.

When she stopped at the gate both men thought that perhaps she had been working on riding Princess and wanted to show them the progress.

They were caught by surprise.

"I know where the thoroughbred belongs.

"I knew there had to be a way to mark them other than a regular brand. She belongs to the Army. She has an identifying mark in her left ear."

"Jed I just thought of something," said Ben.

"A man on the wagon train was talking about the Army tattooing a number inside a horse's ear to identify it." Ben looked in the horse's ear and saw the mark.

"She is "CONNOR US ARMY #7729". Beth is right!"

"This is terrible! Ben I don't want you to give her back. She is the best horse here! They don't need her. They have lots of good horses!"

"We have to Jed. She isn't ours."

"She looks like she could have that foal, any day now. Maybe we should put her in a stall by herself," said Ben.

"We can't give her back!" growled Jed. "We need her to start our herd. Why did you have to go looking in her ear?" Jed walked sullenly away, down the path. He was upset and not at all proud of the way he had reacted. He had counted on her to be the first of many thoroughbreds they would have. Now they had to take time to return her to the army. Ben, too, was sad. He thought the army was probably at the settlement by now. That had to be where she came from.

"I will return her as soon as the foal is strong enough to make the trip," Ben said it to Beth with firm conviction. "I will find out how to do the ear marking when I return her. They must numb it. I want something permanent on the horses without the painful branding on their coats.

He followed Jed to the new barn where they had been working as Beth moved the thoroughbred into a stall and covered the floor of it with fresh hay. She gave her water and patted her rump as she started to leave, the beautiful mare whinnied.

"Are you lonesome, girl? Someone has taken good care of you. You may belong with the Army but you have a spot in some soldier's heart. It is easy to see that you have been loved."

CHAPTER TEN   UNCLE BEN, UNCLE BEN!

The men continued working on Jed's barn but had to include other jobs, too.

Early morning, the next day, Ben and Jed were working on getting stones for Ben's fireplace. Ben was at the hut with Big Boy and a skid, unloading stones into a growing pile near the door when he heard Slim Parker's son, Joshua shouting!

"Uncle Ben, Uncle Ben, the Indians came. They shot my Dad and took Mama and Adam away! I was by the river fishing when the Indians came. I grabbed Dixie and rode her, bareback across the river and hid in the trees.

"They took the workhorses and burned the wagon and our cabin. Oh Uncle Ben, I didn't know what to do, so I rode here. Help me, Uncle Ben! I don't know what to do! They shot my Dad, and he fell off the roof and I've got to find Mama and Adam!"

Joshua had been dry-eyed when he started his message, but now he ran into Ben's arms and burst into heartbroken sobs.

"When Joshua? When did they come? "They came last night when Mama was getting ready for supper. We had three fish and I wanted to catch another one. She had Adam and was looking for greens. My dad was putting the roof on the cabin. He didn't have his rifle up there because it kept sliding and he said if it fell it would go off and hurt someone and Mama forgot to take hers."

"The Indians came. They rode out of the woods so fast that my dad couldn't even get down in time to get to his rifle. I was so scared that I just grabbed Dixie and crossed the river and hid. Mama has been making me swim, and practice crossing on Dixie. I guess it was a good thing. One of the Indians scooped my Mama up onto his horse and rode away. Another one took Adam. What are we going to do Uncle Ben?" The boy had delivered the rest of his story between sobs. His whole body shook.

Jed had been at the riverbank and followed Joshua up to the hut. He stood there with eyes widened by fear, not for himself, but for Beth and Johnny. Jed asked nearly the same question that Joshua did.

"What should we do first?"

"We have to go look for their trail. The longer we wait the harder it will be to follow."

Beth had carried Johnny up the path and when she saw Joshua wrapped in Ben's arms, she feared instantly that the worst had happened.

"What has happened?" She asked. Ben gave her a quick and condensed version.

"Joshua, how did you get here? How did you find us?" she asked.

"I followed the river and looked for the biggest tree with the writing on it." I remembered that from when we all were here, helping to make Uncle Jed's house."

"You have been a very brave boy. You did the right thing. Let's all walk up to the house and decide what must be done."

Jed knew what he wanted to do. He wanted to take Beth and Johnny to the settlement where they would be protected. The soldiers needed to know what had happened. They would help get Mary and Adam back. Ben was thinking along the same lines, but he thought that Jed should go alone as he had before and he should bring some soldiers back with him quickly. Maybe they had an expert tracker that could help.

Beth wiped Joshua's face and hands with a soft piece of leather that she had dipped in cold water. She gave him a big drink of water and held him in her arms for a long time. Tears found their way down her cheeks as she tried to comfort him. She put him on a pallet in Johnny's room and closed the shutters to block the sunlight.

"I doubt if he has slept any since it happened. He is exhausted. I'm hoping that he will sleep now and I will feed him when he wakes."

Ben walked over to the fireplace and doused the fire.

"Until this is over, we can't have any more fires. I'm going to put mine out right now." He started out the door and then he turned around and looked at Jed.

"I think we should not pound any more nails or shoot. No use telling them where we are.

Jed immediately thought of the riverbank near the hut that was dug up where they had been hauling stones out for Ben's fireplace. He hurried after Ben to help repair it and remove any sign that people had been there. They carried every stone inside the hut and brushed away the footprints and marks made by the skid. They filled the pond, took care of the chickens and threw extra bundles of grass into the corral. The area was quiet.

The thoroughbred was down lying on her side. She was about to deliver the foal. The beautiful long legged baby came into the world without incident. She was brown with white feet and a white blaze on her forehead that matched her mother's. After making the stall spotlessly clean, they gave her water and grain and hay. Ben couldn't take his eyes off that pretty new face.

"She is special," said Jed. "You can tell that with one look.

"You're right," said Ben, "but don't get attached. She's not ours remember?"

"I remember," said Jed.

Beth was pacing when they returned.

"What took you so long?"

"We were delivering a baby!" said Jed.

"She's beautiful," said Ben, "and healthy and arrived with no problem. She looks exactly like her mother."

"I will wait until the boys wake up and have had something to eat and then I'll take them to see her. It will give Joshua something to think about besides that nightmare he just went through."

"That's a good idea, Honey."

"Please, from now on, remember to take your gun with you at all times!"

"Don't worry. I will!"

Jed gathered a bundle to take in the canoe, while reminding everyone about the possible use of the tunnel or the "stone room." That was the name they had given the enclosure around the huge boulder in the hut. He said if they had to leave, to go to the little cave.

Once again, he warned about fires and loud noises and said that he was really sorry for the way he had acted about the army's horse.

They joined hands and prayed for protection for Mary and Adam. They prayed for protection for Jed's trip and for the whole family. They thanked God that Joshua had been able to find them, and Jed added, that he was glad that the foal was born without incident.

"I have to go now Beth, be brave Honey, and I love you," he said, holding her close for just an instant.

He took the bundle and his rifle and headed for the hut where his canoe was still stored. It only took him a few minutes to put it in the water and paddle out of sight.

"Ben, I hate this! My stomach is in a knot. How can I bring another baby into a world where we live in fear?"

"You're going to have another baby?" asked Ben.

In her distress, she had given away her well-kept secret.

"I am pretty sure that another one is on the way."

"Beth, that is wonderful! Now don't fret. You know that our place is tucked down in between the bluff and trees and even hard to find if you know it is here. We will keep Joshua busy until the soldiers find his mother. He sounded more confident than he felt.

"Beth, I need to leave you here with the boys and go find Slim. It is possible that he was only wounded. I want you to pack a bundle and go to the hut when Joshua wakes up. Be alert and keep the boys quiet. It would be easier from there to head down river to the cave. If you have to leave here without me, it is on the other side of the river, past the Parker place in a small bluff. I would meet you somewhere along the route. Keep your gun with you at all times. I hate leaving you alone. The alternate plan would be to take all of you back there with me. I don't want to take Joshua back there right now. He has been through a lot already. I'm going to take Big Boy and I will be back before dark. I promise. Don't worry, Beth, we will get through this, with God's help." She nodded. She was trembling so badly that when she tried to pick up a cup of water, she spilled it.

Ben wrapped his arms around her reassuringly.

"Beth, it is going to be alright. We will find Mary and Adam. This fall you will have Melanie to keep you company. You will have lots of things to teach her. Think about this winter and don't be afraid. God is with us." She nodded again. She could hear Johnny waking up.

"I need to go get him so he doesn't wake up Joshua," she said.

"Aunt Beth, I'm up," said Joshua.

"That's good, because after you have something to eat with Johnny, I have a surprise to show you boys."

"I'm going out to saddle Big Boy." Ben made a bundle for the back of the horse. It contained a water bag, medical supplies, a little food and a shovel.

"Beth I'm leaving now, so that I can get back as soon as possible." He hugged all three of them in a group huddle and rode away. "Pray Beth, Pray".

It would be no slow walk for Big Boy this time. He gave him a nudge and a loose rein and the big muscled horse took off, clearing the river in four easy bounds. Ben let him run. Feeling that the horse seemed to know the urgency of the trip, they traveled swiftly. Big Boy continued to gallop until Ben reined him in when the Parker place came in view. It was a nightmare.

"Where is Uncle Ben going?" asked Joshua. "He has gone to check your camp and Uncle Jed has taken his canoe and gone to the settlement to warn them about the Indians and to bring help to search for your mom and Adam."

"First we will all sit at the table and you and I will have a bowl of stew before it gets totally cold, Johnny will have to have his strained into a mush. Then we are going to see the surprise." She tried hard to be brave.

Beth bowed her head to say grace.

"Father, I give thanks for all we have and the wonderful food you have provided. We thank you that Joshua's mother and brother are uninjured and well and that we will soon find them and bring them back safely."

She rolled bedding and diapers into a manageable but heavy bundle and used a strap to put it on her back. She made a smaller bundle for Joshua to carry, filled with food and things they would need if they had to go to the cave. She wiped Johnny's face, and then picked him up. On one arm was Johnny. The gun and water bag were on the other arm. They headed for the hut. By the time she got there, her arms and lower back were aching.

She checked the fire pit and was glad to find a glowing coal. She used it to light a candle. That reminded her to get the firebox and sit it next to the bundles.

"Why did you light the candle now, Aunt Beth? It isn't dark?"

"Because the big fire is going to be out, and it is easy to keep the candle burning. Tonight we can light the lantern from the candle without any problem." The bundles were placed just inside the door.

She carried Johnny and the gun and asked Joshua to close the hut door behind them.

"Our surprise is in the barn." She led the way. The only horses in the barn were the purebreds. The new foal was every bit as lovely as Ben had said.

"Isn't she beautiful?" Beth said. Joshua stepped into the stall beside the new foal. He ran his hand down her back and looked at her face.

"You are a pretty baby," he said. "She looks just like her mother."

He patted the mare on her neck and turned to Beth. "She wasn't here when we were here before. Where did she come from?" he asked.

"She was lost and traveling with the wild horses. When she saw Big Boy she liked him so much that she decided she wanted to follow him home," said Beth. "That's a story isn't it?"

"No, Joshua, it really happened."

"Joshua, do you think you could keep Johnny safe here in the barn and play with him for a few minutes? I want to climb up the bluff so I can see if anyone is around?"

"Sure I can. Sometimes I watch Adam for Mom when she has to do something," said Joshua.

"He likes to play with this leather strap," said Beth. "Let him chew on it. I will be up on the bluff. I will be able to see the barn all the time I am gone, so you aren't really alone. Will that be alright?"

165

"Sure Aunt Beth, don't worry. I won't let him get hurt." She took her gun and hurried up the path they had marked on the bluff. Her back hurt worse now and she was getting bad cramps.

Once she got to the top she sat down. She felt dizzy. She turned left and then right. No movement was in sight, in any direction. She looked again and studied the trees up and down the river. She spotted a deer standing in the shade. You are safe right now. We cannot hunt you, she thought. Her head had cleared and she headed down the path. Once again the dizziness came. She used the rifle to steady herself, as she leaned against the warm rocks behind her until it passed. Just a few more feet down and she could sit down in the barn. Her pain was nearly unbearable.

As soon as she got inside, she crawled onto the pile of hay and lay there.

"Did you see anything, Aunt Beth?"

"I saw a beautiful deer down by the river."

"Aunt Beth you look all funny white. Are you sick?"

"Yes Joshua, I guess I am. I want to go in one of the back stalls and rest for a while. Will you stay with Johnny for a while longer?"

"Sure Aunt Beth." She knew what was happening. She would not be holding a new baby next summer.

The clean hay provided a cushion and the stall walls concealed from the boy's eyes her distress and all that followed. She lay there trying not to give in to the darkness that threatened to overtake her.

"Lord Jesus, help me. I am responsible for these boys. Help me to find the strength to care for them. Help me to know that you are our protector and strength. Please help me!"

When she opened her eyes again, Ben was looking down at her with so much concern and fear in his face that she felt guilty.

"Thank God. You are alive! You are so white and were lying so still that I thought we had lost you." She struggled to sit up but the dizziness and weakness made it impossible.

"Where is Johnny? Where is Joshua? Are they alright?" "They are fine. Joshua took Johnny back to the house and fed him some more of the mush you were feeding him earlier. He is quite a boy."

"I'm not sure what I should do for you!" I'm going to make the tea that Jed made for me when the cougar clawed my shoulder. I'll put lots of willow bark in it. Don't move! Both the boys will be with me. Don't worry. Don't do anything!" He hurried to the front of the barn, scooping Johnny into his arms as he went.

"Come with me, Josh." Joshua had to almost run to keep up.

"Joshua, you have acted like a grown up the past two days. I will never think of you as a little boy again!"

When Ben stepped into the hut, he was glad to see the little flame on the candle at the back of the room. He piled kindling and small branches in the fire pit, lighting them with the candle. He balanced the pan of water on three stones over the little fire. Searching for the right herbs took a few minutes. Things had not been put back in the same places as they had originally been, after the boulder had forced him to rebuild. He found what he was looking for, and crumbled them into the heating water. He took the scrubbed, torn strips of the sheet and the last piece of his mother's skirt and tucked them in his pockets. At the last minute he added the flowers that fight infection to the heating brew. He stuffed a cup in his top pocket.

"Josh, I need you to carry Johnny, if you can. I have to bring the pan of hot tea and a second pan of hot water." He had set the big pan, half full, near the flame to heat. He stuffed two rabbit skins inside his shirt and took a soft deer skin that he had taken the hair off, to make a new shirt.

"I guess I'm ready if you are," said Ben. He looked at the candle and stopped long enough to add grease to it so it wouldn't sputter out. The small cooking fire was nearly out. He had not added any wood to it since the original few branches. He carefully carried the pans to the barn, watching the boy struggle to carry the growing baby with his exhausted muscles.

"Josh, how will I ever thank you for all you have done here today?"

"You don't have to thank me. That's the way it is done out here, right? We help each other. You said so yourself," said Joshua, "when you were talking to Mom, remember?"

"That's right, Josh. We help each other." He scooped out a little of the hot water into a small waterproof basket that Beth had made. It hung on the wall of the barn. Ben added some chamomile to it. He pounded a small piece of jerky from the cache until it was pulp and added that. There, he thought that will steep while I see what I can do for Beth.

He carried the tea and the hot water to the stall where she lay. He dipped some tea into a cup to cool. "Beth I'm back. I have some medicine cooling that should help a little, and I made a pan of warm water so I can help you wash up a bit. He spread the soft hide on a pile of clean hay on the other side of the stall. He lifted her and placed her in the middle of the hide. It frightened him when he saw the quantity of blood she had lost. He quickly covered it with hay in case Joshua would look into the stall. The strips of cloth were used to pack and absorb but did nothing to stop the flow. He encouraged her to drink the entire cup of medicine.

As soon as he put her head back down on the hay, she fell into a deep sleep. He covered her with a soft pelt and left her to tend to the boys.

Johnny was fussing and Ben realized that he needed to nurse. "Josh, was there any of the mush left that Johnny can eat?"

"Yes, but just a little. Do you want me to get it? It is in the hut by the stew. I went and got both of them earlier from our house when Johnny took a little nap."

"I didn't notice it when we were in there. I guess my mind was on just what I was doing. Thanks Josh." Ben added a bit of the warm chamomile mixture to the mush and felt that it was soft enough to offer the baby. He hurried back to the hut returning with a spoon, and two cups. He gave a big piece of jerky to Joshua, and began spooning tiny bites of the mush into Johnny's mouth. He poured some of the chamomile tea into a cup and told Josh that he should drink every bit of it." Joshua sipped it and then drank the whole thing down. Ben poured the rest into the boy's cup. After doing his best to make Johnny comfortable, by using the second rabbit fur to wash him, he used his last strip of cloth to swaddle his bottom.

Before long, both boys were asleep in the hay. Joshua woke twice during the night screaming from his dreams. Each time, Ben knelt beside him praying silently for guidance and help. He wrapped his arms around Joshua and just quietly held him close until the boy went back to sleep.

Beth slept continually unless Ben woke her enough to get her to drink more medicine or broth. He had removed the stained hay and all that it held, during the night and buried it near the side of the barn beside Bold One, marking the spot with three large rocks. At first light he made a second pan of medicine and while he had the small fire going, he ground grain and meat and cooked a huge batch of meal. He left the boys, just long enough to climb up the path on the bluff three times. The last time he went up, it was nearly dark again. He was relieved that they had made it through the second day without any further problems.

He discovered with relief, the diapers in the bundles that morning. He had run out of things he could use on the tyke's bottom. The caches in the hut provided, more than ample rations for them. Ben had given Joshua a large bowl of the meal, adding nuts and honey.

"This is good, Uncle Ben. You need to eat some, too." Ben realized he hadn't eaten in two days. He didn't feel like eating, but knew that he had to keep his mind and body capable of taking care of Beth and the boys.

"Ben, can you hear me?" Beth's voice was very weak. Ben rushed to her side. "Please bring Johnny here and lay him beside me so that he can nurse. I need for him to nurse." Ben knew that having the baby against her would be a comfort, but he didn't know the ways of nursing mothers. Johnny nursed greedily. He cuddled in his mother's arms and with a full tummy he went back to sleep.

"You need more medicine." He offered her the cup and she took sips without disturbing the baby.

"I think I am doing a little better. I don't feel quite so dizzy," she whispered.

"That is wonderful news. If I bring you some broth, will you try to drink a little?" He didn't expect an answer. He lifted her head and helped her sip the broth. She said she was tired and closed her eyes. Joshua walked over near the stall, and asked if she was going to be all right.

"With God's help, I think so. She is still very sick, Josh. We need to let her rest as much as she can. Let's go out and check on the animals. We can give this purebred some attention, when we come back in."

When they stepped out of the barn, Ben was surprised to see that it was afternoon.

"Josh, would you throw some of the hay bundles in the corral? Do you think you can get it up and over the fence? It is pretty high."

"I'll try Uncle Ben."

"While you are doing that, I am going to go up on the bluff again," said Ben. "I won't be long." He came down with a small smile, and said, "All clear Josh."

"I like it when you call me Josh instead of Joshua. It feels friendly like," said Joshua, with a smile. Ben couldn't help but chuckle.

"You are my friend Josh. You are like a little brother." The boy wrapped his arms around Ben's middle and hugged him tight. Ben decided that keeping the boy busy would help him to fight the tears that were trying to escape. Ben tossed two more bundles of hay into the corral.

"I could only get one in there. They are too heavy," said Josh.

172

"Let's take care of the chickens and see if they have laid any eggs," Ben said. They found five. I knew we hadn't gathered them for a couple days. Some of the younger ones must be starting to produce, he thought. He filled the pond and told Joshua to watch Rusty. Before it was half filled, the horse was in the water stomping and splashing.

"He does that every time we fill the pond," said Ben.

"He sure likes water," said Joshua with a laugh. Ben had put Dixie in the corral with the rest of the horses before he left. She was eating hay and had turned to the pond to watch Rusty, too.

Ben carried the candle into the barn and brought his Bible. He sat beside the open door in the light and read from 1 Corinthians 15:20-58.NIV. Joshua listened closely to the words. He didn't understand all of it but he knew that it promised that his father would live again. As Ben read the words, he too, felt strengthened in the promise of life to come.

Joshua seemed restless.

"Uncle Ben does all that mean that my dad will live again?" He wanted to hear Ben say it in his own words.

"Yes, Josh, he will be raised up and live in heaven." It was quiet in the barn. Josh sat down near the small fire beside Ben. "You will see your dad again someday."

"I forgot about your supper. We fed the animals but I didn't fix you anything. Will you settle for jerky and berry leather?" He slipped his arm around the boy's shoulder as he asked him.

"Sure. I was just wondering where Mama and Adam are and if they are alright." He hesitated for a moment and then asked, "Uncle Ben, did you bury my Dad?"

"Yes, Josh. I did."

"Where did you bury him?"

"I put him near the path to the spring," said Ben, "under the tallest pine tree." "Did you put writing on the tree?"

"No. I just put a cross. I thought you might want to do that yourself when you are a little older."

"Thanks, Uncle Ben." Ben was amazed at the understanding in the young boy's mind. "Is it alright if I go and sit by the river for a while?" asked Joshua. "I'll be careful. I promise."

"Sure, go ahead."

It was quite dark when Joshua came back in the barn and without saying a word; he curled up in the same spot that he had slept on before. Ben could see that Joshua had been crying. It will take a long time for him to deal with all this, Ben thought. He quietly picked up Johnny and changed his diaper, fed him some mush and put him on a pallet in the hay near Joshua.

He had cups of medicine and broth ready when Beth began to stir. He spoke quietly and got her to take some of each. She said she wanted Johnny back, but he told her that he was fed and dry and asleep with Joshua. She smiled and closed her eyes.

Joshua woke everyone in the middle of the night screaming. Ben held him cradled in his arms until morning.

It was raining. Ben heard Johnny start to fuss. He picked him up and opened the shutters on one of the windows just enough so that they could look out. As the rain hit the babies hand he looked wide eyed and surprised.

When, after a few minutes, he started to fuss again, Ben changed his diaper and carried him over to see the baby horse. He was really too young to appreciate the rain or the horse, but Ben hoped that new sights, might entertain him until Beth woke naturally.

"Ben, bring him to me," said Beth. "There is only one thing that he wants right now." She cuddled him and he was content patting her face as he nursed.

Joshua stretched and went out in the rain, without a word. He came back after a little while.

"They are coming, just like in my dream." Ben's heart lurched and nearly stopped.

"Who is coming?"

"The soldiers are coming, riding hard. They are coming fast. Uncle Jed is in front."

"How do you know that?" asked Ben. "I climbed up the bluff and I could see them."

"You shouldn't climb up there. You might fall and get hurt. The rocks are wet and slippery now. That makes it even harder."

"It wasn't hard and I was careful," said Joshua.

Jed brought the soldiers across the river and right up in front of the hut. Ben rushed out of the barn to meet them.

"We came as fast as we could," said Jed as he swung down from a brown horse."

"Major Connors, this is my brother, Ben Slater."

"How do you do, Sir?" said Ben. He turned and introduced Joshua Parker to the Major. "It was Joshua's family that the Indians raided," said Ben.

"I see," said the Major. "Are you alright son?"

"Yes sir, I am. It's Aunt Beth that's sick."

"Beth? Where is she? What happened? What's the matter with her?"

"Calm down Jed, she is in the barn. Go in quietly or you will wake Johnny."

Jed hurried into the barn leaving the big door wide open. The Major glanced in that direction and when he did he could see My Girl and her new foal.

"That's my horse," he stormed. "You have my horse!"

"Yes Sir, we do. She has had good care and she has a beautiful foal."

"How did you get her?"

"That's a long story for another time. What's important right now is that we find this boy's mother and little brother." The Major looked apologetic.

"I understand the boy lost his father. I'll send a detail to bury him."

"That won't be necessary. I took care of that myself. He was a good man and my friend."

The Major looked at Ben for a moment and then said that he had a detail of scouts return with information about a tribe of Indians settled on the other side of the wagon trail beyond the big rock country.

"Maybe they have the woman and her son. I think we should try there first," said the Major.

"What if they don't have her?"

"Then we will have to figure out something else. It's a sure thing that this rain has washed away any trail they might have left."

"Major, are you willing to wait for a few minutes while I talk to Jed? I want to ride out with you."

"Sure but don't take very long." Joshua followed Ben into the barn. Beth was still holding Johnny and she and Jed were talking.

"Jed, I'm sorry I have to interrupt. I only have a few minutes. I'm going to ride out with the Major."

Before he picked up his gun and Big Boy's saddle, he tried to explain what he had put in the medicine and how ill Beth had really been. He told Jed that Joshua had been a man and taken care of Johnny and Beth while he was away, taking care of matters at the Parker homestead. He held Joshua's hand and Jed's as he closed his eyes to gather his thoughts.

"Thank you, Lord, for being here with us at this moment," said Ben. "Thank you that Beth is regaining her strength, and please Father; watch over my family while I am gone with the soldiers to find Mary and Adam. Lord, please ride with me and make our search successful. Let us find them quickly and in good health. Thank you, Lord. Amen."

Ben picked up a water bag and hugged Joshua. He stepped into the hut just long enough to make a bedroll and to grab his old hide that he used for a tent when he went hunting. With his water bag hanging from the saddle horn, he crammed a saddlebag full of jerky and made sure the other one had plenty of shells for his favorite rifle. At the last minute he took two of the bone knives he had made and wrapped them in a rabbit's fur and pushed them in on top of the shells. He was thinking he might offer them in trade for Mary and Adam. He was willing to promise much more.

As soon as he put the saddle on Big Boy, he was ready. The last thing he did was to stick his head in the barn and remind Jed to take extra special care of the Major's horses, and to brush away all the visible horse prints after they left. The Major looked at Ben and smiled.

"You are a take charge type young man aren't you?"

"Yes Sir, I guess I am," answered Ben. "I have had to be."

"Did you ever think of joining the Army?"

"No Sir, I never did."

They rode across the river, out from under the big oak tree and onto the prairie in a straight line for the wagon trail. The Major had no idea what he would do when he got to the Indian camp. He rode along silently setting a brisk pace. He feared the longer they took the less chance they had of finding the captives. The rain continued for another hour and then finally quit, allowing the sun to dry their clothes and the prairie grass.

Big Boy enjoyed being able to stretch into a fast pace. He was strong and his muscles were used to traveling. Now that Ben had gotten familiar with his ways, he appreciated the big horse and the stamina and power he had. When they stopped for a break, he showed no signs of being tired.

"That's a good horse you're on, but he is pretty marked up. Who used the spurs on him?" asked the Major, as they headed out again this time at a slower pace. Ben told the Major the whole story of the settlement coming and the drifter trying to steal Buddy.

He told about Bold One and then about Slim shooting her.

Next, he told about Big Boy and about his first ride on him and getting bucked over his head. From there he branched into the story of Big Boy fighting the Stallion to keep Ginger, and ending up with My Girl and the brown filly too. Finally he told him about Sarah and the Indian raid on his family and that he hoped to go find her soon.

"Ben I have never met a young man with as many good stories to tell. I sure appreciate the good care you gave My Girl. She is more like a pet to me than a mount. I guess I have always treated her differently. Sometimes I know some of the men think I'm crazy, the way I baby her. I sure have missed her."

"Major it was a pleasure to have her around. We think she is the finest horse we have ever seen."

"Son, she probably is. That horse cost a small fortune. She is bred to race. We have never stayed one place long enough to train her properly, but you should see her run!" Ben enjoyed watching the Major's face as he talked about his horse. It was obvious that he loved her and was proud of her.

"There's a slight ridge up ahead. I think we should camp on this side of it for tonight." He ordered his men to make camp, with no fire. "It could be dangerous to let anyone know we are here," he said. The men groaned as they spread out their bedrolls. They knew that no fire meant they would have no coffee before they started out in the morning. Two men were ordered to stand guard.

Another shift of two was assigned to take over at an appointed time. They had a quiet, cold meal and then the camp slept.

The soldiers were surprisingly efficient, and quiet at breaking camp in the morning when the Major. gave the order. They headed out in a column of two's just before sunrise. Once again the Major set a fast pace. He wanted to reach the woods mentioned in the report. The ground was dusty and dry now. There was no evidence of the rain they had ridden through the day before. Huge boulders that looked like they had been piled by a giant's hand were visible in the distance.

Mid-morning, the Major called a break and the men were more than happy to dismount. Several horses in the column had carried supplies instead of men, and now Ben noticed that the horses were all being watered from barrels. Big Boy did not wait to be led over to the water. He nudged his way up to the barrel and took his drink before many of the others.

"He is making sure he gets his," laughed the Major.

Each horse was given a measured amount of grain. "Give the big guy extra. I have a feeling he burns up more than the others," said the Major as he strolled over to the shade of a rock and sat down to chew on some jerky. Ben walked over and rubbed Big Boy with some harsh grass he had collected.

"I doubt if they could eat that stuff, but it makes a good brush," he said, as one of the soldiers nearby, started doing the same for his mount. "I wonder how long it will be before we see the Indian camp," commented Ben.

"I think Major Connors will tell us before much longer," answered the young soldier.

They rode out soon after, finding it much more comfortable. A cloud cover had cooled the sky and cut the glare.

It was late afternoon when they entered the trees. For the first time, the major pulled a hand drawn map from his pocket. He studied it quietly, folded it carefully and then put it back away. They rode into the woods a short distance. The smell of water attracted Big Boy's attention. Before long, all the horses were gathering around a beautiful pond formed by a spring that bubbled out of the rocks above it.

"We will wait here," said Major Connors. He assigned sentry duty and sent a small party out ahead, to cautiously see what they could. Most of the soldiers took the opportunity to eat and rest. One bent down near the pond and picked up a thumb nail sized blue stone. He rubbed it clean and tucked it into his trouser pocket smiling. He was pleased with his small treasure.

After a short time the scouts returned saying that they had seen a few animals, but not much else. The trees are thick and follow the bluff for a long ways.

Major Connor nodded.

"We will stay here until first light. C. Q. Private Anderson and take first watch. Private Johnson, take second watch."

"Yes Sir," they acknowledged at the same time.

"Private, I'm Ben Slater."

"Private James Anderson, Sir. Anything I can do for you Sir?"

"No, I don't need anything, but you can tell me what the Major meant by C.Q."

"That just means cold and quiet. Like last night. No fires and no talking above a soft whisper, and no noise."

"Thanks, said Ben, nice meeting you."

CHAPTER ELEVEN   WHO GOES THERE?

Mary was occupied with staying on the horse, holding Adam safely in front of her and trying to recite her route in her head. The dense trees didn't allow the moonlight to filter through enough to let her see the sentry leaning against a tree. She rode into the midst of the sleeping soldiers before she knew that they were there. He shouted.

"Who goes there?" He startled her and her horse. Instantly waking everyone, as Ben ran to her and scooped Mary and Adam from the nervously prancing horse and held them close. She was laughing and crying at the same time.

"I can't believe you are real! How did you find me?" Mary asked with tears streaming down her face.

"Joshua came down the river on Dixie and told us what happened. He is safe with Jed and Beth. The major stepped up to introduce himself and to answer her question.

"I am Major Connors from the new fort where the Hickory and Silver rivers join. We had a report that Indians had a village on the other side of the woods. When Jed told us about the raid and that you had been taken, I decided that the village might be a good place to start looking."

Ben reached over and took Adam from her arms. Mary looked exhausted. He glanced at the horse and noted the handmade saddle, the furs and the rifle sticking out of them. It was apparent that someone had helped her. He wondered who in an Indian village would help a captive to escape.

"Thank you, Lord, for helping them," he said.

The Major was glad that he did not have to go into the village to look for them. He loved happy endings. But then he remembered, from the report that there might be another white person in that camp. He needed to know who it was. Maybe he did need to go into their camp, but he couldn't do it now.

"They will be looking for you and the child. We need to get you away from here." he said. The barrels were refilled with fresh water from the little pool. The horses had rested and had been allowed to drink freely. They had munched the sweet grass and were ready to go. The men had refreshed their water bags and they were eager to head back.

Ben, Mary and Major Connors, rode three abreast in front of the column as soon as they cleared the trees and rode out onto the prairie.

"Mary, where do you want to go?" asked the Major. "You can't go back to your homestead. They didn't leave anything there." She told the Major that she didn't know where she would end up, but she had to go to Ben's to get her son.

"That's fine because I want to go there to see my horse before I return to the fort," he said.

Beth was up and feeling much better by the time the soldiers rode in with Ben, Mary and Adam.

185

Joshua hugged his mother and wouldn't let go. Then he hugged Adam the same way.

"I prayed that Jesus would help them find you. He did Mama. He answered my prayer," said Joshua.

"He answered all our prayers," said Beth.

"We have a lot to be thankful for," said Jed, as he slipped his arm protectively around Beth's tiny waist.

"Well I sure do," said Major Connors. "I want to see My Girl, if it's alright."

"Sure," said Ben. When Ben looked in the barn door a few minutes later, the Major was standing with his forehead against My Girl and his arms wrapped around her neck.

"If I didn't know better, I would think he is crying," said Ben quietly to Jed. Jed peeked in and came back.

"As long as the Army is taking her away, I am glad that Major Connor is the one who owns her.

Beth told the cook for the group that he could make a fire up in front of the house by the lake, and that she had lots of dried vegetables that would be good for a stew. She would soon have a lot more with the huge garden they had in and growing. He was pleased to finally have a chance to cook a good meal for the men. They had not had a fire in many days. He brewed plenty of strong coffee and baked wonderful biscuits to go with the stew. It seemed almost like a picnic with the soldiers there. Mary, Joshua, Adam and Ben all sat on one blanket. Nearby were Jed, Beth and Johnny.

Mary was so happy to see and talk to Beth again.

"If the rest were as nice as the Indian girl with blue eyes no one would have a problem with them."

"What did you just say, Mary?" asked Ben and the Major at the same time.

"She is the one I told you about. Remember? Her name is Brave Sparrow and she helped me to escape. I told you about her while we were riding. The Chief was going to let a warrior named Growling Bear claim me as his wife at the end of the full moon. I stayed in her tent. It was bigger than all the rest. I asked her why it was and she said it was because she was their healer and the tent was used for communal meetings. She was taller than me, thin and quite pretty. I didn't like her hair. It looked dull and sort of chalky as if she had it coated with something."

"Do you think she could be white?" asked the Major.

"Yes she is white. She told me that they brought her there when she was a little girl. She is the adopted daughter of Chief Dark Wolf."

Ben felt a renewal of the feeling he had always had that one day he might find Sarah. He wanted to ask the Major to go back with him right that second, but something stopped him. If she could help Mary to come back, why didn't she just come back here too, if she was Sarah? He failed to realize that she thought he was killed, all those long years ago. She was so young when they took her from her parent's wagon. She had no way of knowing that the very route that Mary followed could lead her back to her brother and a new life.

*****

Jed, Ben and the Major, stood in a group around My Girl.

"I appreciate you taking such good care of her and the foal for me. I'll send for them when I'm sure that she and the little one can travel without any stress on them. In the mean time I'll have your canoe returned to you so that it will be here if you should need it. If you need us, just send for us like you did before. You have a great location here and I think you will be undetected for a long time. It should be fine to hunt and have a fire if you make it a habit to use the bluff for a look out post and check the area faithfully."

The soldiers were mounted and just before he gave the order to move out, Major Connor looked at the horse that Jed had used on the ride back from the fort. I think she likes it here. If you care to keep her, she will help pay for the care you are giving My Girl and her foal. The Major swung up as he bid good-bye to everyone.

"Sir, we didn't expect pay. She is a pleasure to have around."

"Yes, well, Sally is staying and that's an order! She is about four years, and has had one nice foal. She is a good mount, smooth and doesn't tire quickly. Maybe you can get her together with that big fella over there."

Misses Parker, you are welcome to come and stay at the fort until someone is heading back the way you came. Good Luck to you and the boys. Move um out!" He smiled and waved as the column headed for the crossing near the big oak.

"God bless you Major," said Mary, "Thank you again, for everything," she called out loudly.

"Mary, I am so glad that you have decided to stay here with us at least for a while," said Beth. "It will be nice to have a woman to talk to. It is impossible for you to know what you want to do but just take it a day at a time for now. Right now, I think we girls need to go up to the house and have a cup of tea."

As they headed for the house, Beth smiled at the men heading for the unfinished barn.

"No doubt the men will be back working on the barn before the water is hot."

Stump came bounding up to Beth as they passed the wolf den. He nearly knocked her over. In one swoop he licked Adam's face and nuzzled Mary's hand for a scratch.

"Well hello. Where have you been for such a long time?" asked Beth. She was happy that he was back and in good shape. Adam reached for him saying,

"Kitty, Kitty,"

"No Adam, this is Stump. He is a dog. Say doggie."

189

"Doggie," said Adam struggling in Mary's arms to reach and grab Stump's fur.

"I can't wait for Johnny to start talking." Stump headed off in the direction of the new barn where Jed, Joshua and Ben stood talking.

As the women entered the house the men were receiving enthusiastic greetings from Stump.

They had decided to convert Ginger's old area in the hut into a fresh clean bedroom for Mary and Adam. They pulled everything out. The big door stood wide open.

"We should take the leather flaps down and just leave the wooden door," said Ben.

"Yes," said Jed, "I agree and let's cut a window in the side wall and make a shutter for it like the one on the bedroom on the other side."

"They will need beds."

"It looks like we have plenty to do. We might as well get to it."

"Where do you want to put your coat and boots now that this isn't an entry anymore?" asked Jed.

"I could use one of the branches we cut, just trim it up and put it near the front door for a clothes tree. Let's pick one that is long enough to fasten tight to the ceiling. We might as well get three and put one in each bedroom also. That will get most of the stuff out of the main room," said Ben.

"Good idea," said Jed. "I should do that in our place by the front door."

"Let's take both Ginger and Angel and that way we can bring back the clothes poles, wood for the window frame and shutters and the beds at the same time. Look at Big Boy nuzzling Sally. He figures any of the mares on this ranch are automatically his!"

Just before they left for the woods they both went up the path to the top of the bluff and stood looking out at the prairie. The column of soldiers appeared as tiny dots heading for the wagon trail. When they scanned up and down, Jed spotted the deer that Beth had seen days earlier, grazing in the shade near the river.

"Let's get him first and that will give the girls something to concentrate on. It will be good to keep them both busy for a while."

"Josh, do you want to go with us?" asked Ben.

The boy was delighted to be included.

"Ask your mom. We will wait right here." As they brought Ginger, Angel, and Dixie, from the corral, Big Boy stomped with impatience when he saw that he would be left behind.

"Sorry Big Boy, but I won't need to take you this time."

"It sure is nice to be able to spot the game from up there. It makes hunting a lot easier." They crossed the river and walked the horses as quietly as possible. They had explained to Joshua that he shouldn't talk until the deer was down.

It didn't take long to bring the deer back to the river crossing on the travois, and load it on the raft. Ginger was an old hand at helping and pulled the raft across and held it firmly against the bank, where the deer was transferred to the skid they had used for the stones. The girls were surprised to see the horses coming up the path so soon with the big deer in tow.

Mary commented on the possibility for Ben to make another pair of decorated antlers.

"I love the ones you made for Jed," she said. "I saw them in the house, when we had tea. Ben certainly has a lot of talents, doesn't he?" said Mary as they set to work on the meat.

Jed fed the fire for Beth that the soldiers had used and brought up the drying racks. Ben skinned it and removed the entire head, and then cut the antlers off much the same way he had before. He took them to the edge of the lake and scrubbed them with sand, feeling pleasure at hearing the compliment from Mary.

"I will clean these with salt later. Is there anything else that I can do for you girls before we head to the woods?" Ben asked. "We need to get some wood."

"No but aren't you hungry? You should probably eat before you go," offered Beth.

"We will take some jerky with us and eat a meal with you girls tonight. Don't work too hard," said Jed, with his eyes focusing on Beth's. She nodded and smiled, but her smile faded as she saw the tears silently streaming down Mary's face.

As the men rode slowly away, Mary could no longer restrain her tears.

"Beth, what will I do without Slim? I loved him so much. He was a good man. What will we do? Who will raise the boys? We had such wonderful plans. It was all for them, but now it was all for nothing! They will miss him so much. I miss him, Beth. I didn't get to say Good bye!" It's my fault, Beth. I didn't have my gun with me! He told me to always carry it. It's my entire fault that he is gone." She started to sob and Beth knew that Mary had not had a chance to talk about Slim, or to grieve. Beth wrapped her arms around Mary and rocked back and forth trying to comfort her.

"I know Mary. I lost James after just a couple months of Marriage. It is hard to be tough. You can't hold all your tears in. It's all right to cry. I cried lots of times until I had no more tears. You are not alone, dear friend. We love you and will do anything we can to help you and the boys. You need to put it out of your mind that you had any part in his death. You were outnumbered and caught off guard. You can't blame yourself any more than I can take the blame for the raid on the wagon train."

Beth could see that Adam was starting to be stressed by Mary's crying. She took him from Mary's arms, and entered the house, giving Mary time for her tears. Beth fed Adam and put him down for a nap on the same pallet that Joshua had used. He was safe and comfortable there. He went to sleep quickly. Beth wiped her own tears away, as she came out the front door. She had wanted a brother or sister for Johnny. She was fighting her own loss.

The most precious thing in the world to her heart was to have a big family that loved the Lord and each other.

As they headed to the woods behind the house where the logs had been cut, Ben and Jed could see the women were huddled together, near the fire and they instinctively knew that Mary had started to grieve.

"It is good for them to have each other to talk to. They liked each other right from the start," said Jed. "Beth hasn't said much but I know she has tears bottled up over all that happened.

As the men worked selecting the branches and pieces they would need for the planned projects, Joshua collected a large bundle of firewood, which he piled on top of an old hide and then rolled it into a bundle for Dixie's back.

"Uncle Ben, if you will help me put this on Dixie's back and tie it, I will take it up to help them keep the fire going.

"That will help a lot Josh, remember to be careful."

"I will and I will come right back," he said, as he led Dixie out of the woods toward the fire. The men looked at each other in amazement.

"Did you tell him to do that?" asked Ben.

"No, I thought maybe you had. He is quite a boy. I am growing very fond of him, for many reasons," said Ben. "He is young, but he seems wise beyond his years."

They hauled the wood to the hut without stopping the horses to talk to the woman. They waved as they went by and could see that more than half of the meat was already hanging on the racks. Jed automatically thought of the foaming grease and stretched his hand open wide and closed it into a fist and then opened extra wide again, exercising the tight pink scarred skin that the burn had left.

As soon as he reached the hut, he unhooked Angel and jumped on her back and went back to the women to remind them to keep the grease well back from the fire. He asked if they needed anything and returned in time to help unload most of the wood.

When Ben and Jed saw Joshua coming they could tell where he had been. He had failed to come back to the woods after delivering the firewood.

"I knew that it had been a long time since anyone went up to the look out so I went up," said Joshua. "I wanted to make sure we had an all clear. Guess what I saw! There is a herd of wild horses just the other side of the trees on the other side of the river. Gosh they are beautiful."

"Yes they are," said Jed, "but they can be dangerous. Would you mind going over to the house to tell the women to be on the lookout in case the horses cross the river. Tell them to keep the babies where they can scoop them up and run inside with them."

"I will, Uncle Jed. I'll be right back."

"You said that last time," said Ben.

"Sorry, Uncle Ben but when I remembered that we need to check the look out, I thought it was more important than more firewood."

"It was," said Ben.

"When you come back we will tell you all about what we are making."

Joshua ran down the path to find Stump hot on his heels. The men could hear Josh laugh as he rolled on the grass when the big dog tackled him.

"I hope he delivers our message,"

"It is good to hear him laugh after all that has happened." In a few minutes he came back up the path with Stump and Rascal.

"I told them Uncle Jed. They said thanks for the warning and that you and Uncle Ben can have the heart and liver for your meal."

"That sounds good to me," said Jed.

"Josh have you seen Sunshine today?"

"Yes, she is sleeping in the shade by the house."

"Good. If the horses cross the river she will warn the women in plenty of time."

They removed the leather strips that hung across Ginger's big doorway and had Joshua put them in the barn. Jed cut the hole for the window while Ben stood inside and pounded in supports for the loosened branches that formed the wall. They built the window frame and made it deep in the shape of a box to hold the sod in place, then the shutters. It was nearly dark before they had the shutters finished. Ben wasn't satisfied to stop until he had raked out every stem of grass and made sure that the floor was fresh by turning or replacing the dirt and packing it again. He left the big door and the shutters open.

"It won't hurt to air it out," he said.

"We can start the beds tomorrow. For tonight Mary and Adam can use my bed and I will sleep in the barn with Josh," said Ben. He was not only thinking of trying to accommodate Mary but also he was trying to spare her the pain of hearing Joshua cry out with his bad dreams. He hoped that now she and Adam were back that the dreams would diminish soon. He knew that he couldn't fill the void that Slim had left in their lives but he did hope to give them most of what they needed.

In the next few days the men were able to make three beds. They paled by comparison to the cradle that had been carved and sanded and oiled, but they were strong and serviceable. Ben had made his that way, no carving and nothing fancy. The bark was peeled away, the branches sanded and oiled and the beds were constructed to last for a lifetime.

Two more days and they had made a large trunk for Beth and one for Mary to put at the foot of their beds. Jed made a third one, but it had no lid. That one was made of birch. He set it near the big fireplace in the kitchen of his house to use for wood.

"When the weather turns cold and I get bored, I can carve deer and elk on the wood box to go with the beautiful antlers you made," said Jed.

"It won't be long before we have to start picking and drying vegetables," said Beth, "Mary and I plan to trade some of them at the Trading Post for cloth and thread. We both could use some clothes and the boys are outgrowing theirs."

As days stretched into weeks, Ben's hut had its new fireplace. Finally they were able to walk in without avoiding the huge pile of rocks he and Jed had hastily thrown in the front door, when Joshua had arrived with the news about the Indian raid.

They fell into a routine. Mary and the boys had become more comfortable in their surroundings. Joshua had taken it on himself to be full time look out. He loved it on the top of the bluff and was up there so often that Ben threatened to move his bed up there. Ben had told him that he had sat up there and carved the little figure of the bear. Joshua wanted to learn how to do it.

"All I can say is find a piece of wood that isn't too hard and you will need a knife that has a sharp small blade and just try. Be careful not to slice your hand. The smaller the shavings, the better the figure will look when you are done, and always draw the blade away from you."

Mary heard them talking and told Joshua that she had something very special for him.

"Ben brought this back after he buried your daddy. He gave it to me. I want you to have it." She put the small jackknife in the boy's palm. He recognized it as being his father's right away.

"Oh thank you Mom, I will take good care of it and not lose it. When I use it, I will think about when dad used it."

Mary had washed the hand woven blanket that Brave Sparrow had put under the saddle of the horse. She and Beth had pulled on it and blocked it to prevent shrinking of the wool. Now it lay across the bottom of Adams bed. It will remind me of her, she thought. The rifle hung high on the wall above her bed along with the small-decorated leather pouch that had held the dried grapes. Her bed was covered with the big bearskin that she had worked and reworked until it was beautiful and soft. She had brushed the fur until it was clean and shiny. Beth had woven a large rectangular grass mat that covered most of the floor. The saddle hung in the barn with the others.

Mary had oiled and polished it many times. Ben teased her that if she ever tried to use it again she would probably slide right off. They both chuckled at his joke. Laughter came a little easier as time passed.

CHAPTER TWELVE   THE HONOR OF HELPING

Ben and Jed finally found time to finish Jed's barn and late one Saturday afternoon they told the girls to come out to the barn. They had finished the fence for the corral!

"How on earth did you finish that fence so quickly?" asked Beth.

"We had God's help and Joshua. We couldn't have finished as soon without either one of them," said Jed.

"Ladies, we have all the stalls in the barn ready to receive the horses. We thought since you have put up with being neglected all the time we worked on it, that you might like the honor of helping bring the horses in for the first time!" said Ben. Beth laughed and handed Johnny to Jed.

"I am going to be the first one in the barn and I'm bringing Princess." She laughed all the way down the path as she ran ahead of the others.

"Sometimes she acts like a young girl," said Jed as he admired the beautiful woman running down the path ahead of him.

Jed took Angel and Surprise and walked behind Beth with Johnny on his right arm and the leads in his left hand. He put Angel and Surprise in stalls right beside each other.

"Jed we should move the little brown one, too," said Ben as he moved Sally in the next stall. "Beth can work with her the way she has Princess. That will still leave me with five horses plus I have Dixie and the hunting pony that Mary was riding."

"Are you sure?" asked Jed. "You are the one that caught her."

"I'm sure," said Ben, "but give the poor little girl a name. She is so quiet and hangs out in the back corner. I think she will be better away from Big Boy."

"I can't figure out why a little mouse like that would choose to stay there with him and not go with the herd," said Jed.

"It is strange isn't it? Maybe she found the herd even more frightening."

Jed put a rope on her neck and started to lead her to the new barn.

"Can I take Little Mouse?" asked Joshua.

"I guess so," said Jed, "but watch her close. She is still wild. If she gets frightened or startled she might kick you. We haven't had time to work with her at all."

"I scratch her every day," said Joshua. "I like her a lot," he said.

They watched the boy leading the young horse down the path, jabbering to her as they went.

"I guess she has a name now. It's Little Mouse."

"I like it," said Jed.

After they had eaten the evening meal of fried rabbit and steamed vegetables, they sat on the grass outside and watched Adam playing with a ball. Sunshine would grab it and run around and Adam would laugh out loud.

"Ball, Sun. Ball, Sun." He said. Everyone was surprised by his new words.

"Uncle Ben would you read for us? Read the same part that you did when we were in the barn and Aunt Beth was sick. Remember?" asked Joshua.

"Yes I remember. I read 1 Corinthians chapter 15 verses 20-58 NIV. Why do you want me to read that again, Josh?"

"Because it says my Dad will be raised up with a new body and lives in heaven. I like to think about that." Ben read it for Joshua and God used it to help start to heal and sooth Beth and Mary's hearts, too.

"We will all be together again someday, Joshua," she said. "Your Daddy loves us and he will be there to meet us when we die."

"Ben buried Dad's body near the path to the spring. He marked the tree with a cross. Someday when I can write better, I want to go back there and write on that tree. You can come with me, Mom."

"Yes son, we will do it together. We will see your dad's grave when we go down to harvest our garden."

Early in August, two soldiers arrived and said they had orders to take My Girl to the fort. They read from a paper that looked official. This is from Major Connors.

"Greetings, to Jedidiah Jones, and Benjamin Slater, "You are to keep the foal. I know you will care for her and treat her like the treasure that she is." The soldier continued to read. "I have gotten orders and will be moving out soon and can't take the little one with me. Come as soon as possible so you can get her legal papers. I think that's all. Oh, and one more thing. Ben you should consider joining the Army." Ben laughed at the last remark. "Thank you again for taking good care of My Girl. Best Regards." It was signed by Major Connors.

He was smiling from ear to ear when the soldiers led My Girl across the river and headed back to Fort Connor. The foal cried to its mother and she turned and tried to go back to her. She is bigger than the ones we caught. I guess she will have to learn to eat mash, he thought. I can't wait to tell Jed.

He hurried down the path in time to see Jed heading for the new barn.

"Jed, wait."

"What's going on?" asked Jed. "I have a new project for you," said Ben with a grin.

"Do you really think I need you thinking up new projects? I have two women doing that already!" They both laughed at his remark.

"I think you will like this one. Come over to my barn." Ben opened his barn door. "She needs a name and papers to prove she is ours and she also needs to learn to eat mash."

"I heard the dogs bark, but I didn't hear the soldiers ride in. Wow! They left the foal here for us?"

"Yes they did, Jed"

"I can't believe our good luck!" said Jed.

"I think it is not luck, Jed. I think it is God showing us that He wants our dreams of a thoroughbred ranch to come true."

"I have got to go tell Beth, should I take her with me? No, that's silly. She can stay there for a while. She is used to that stall."

"I'm so excited!"

He hugged Ben and hurried down the path to the house. He stopped short before he entered.

"God, forgive me for what I said about wanting to keep My Girl, when I first saw her. She was your way of giving us the foal. Thank you. Thank you!"

Ben left the next morning for the settlement, to visit the fort and to get a paper saying that the foal "Blaze" was owned by Ben Slater and Jedidiah Jones. Of course he intended to visit Melanie, too. He hurried Big Boy along the trail and sang his way there. At night he couldn't sleep. His heart was light. He was anxious to see the woman he planned to marry.

When he neared the settlement, he could hear hammering and the sounds of construction. More houses had been built since he had been there. Others were under construction.

A church was being built at the edge of town. Someone explained that it was also going to be used as the school for now. Reverend Brown had decided not to ride the circuit anymore. He had moved to the settlement to stay. He was building a house behind the church, just around the corner. Ben noted the new street that meandered to the edge of the Hickory in the distance.

Ben went first to the fort to see the Major. They had a good talk and Ben thanked Major Connor profusely for the foal. He received the paperwork he needed for Blaze and also for Sally. He was instructed on the painless way they put the numbers in the horse's ears. He carefully wrote it all down. They shook hands and ended up hugging each other.

"That was very unmilitary," said Major Connor laughing. "I like the name Blaze that you gave the foal. When it is time, be very selective who you use to start your ranch bloodline."

"Yes sir we will."

"I hope to see you again someday young man. It's been a pleasure."

As Ben left Fort Connor, he eagerly rode on down the Silver to visit the Briggs family. It was good that he had come when he did. Major Connor said he was leaving the next morning. His replacement, Major Benet had arrived that same day. Ben rode along the route of the Silver noticing that many of the largest trees near the water had been cut. He also noticed a number of gardens had been planted leaving strips of cut grass to separate them. Each had a tall stick with the family name on it. That's a good idea, he thought they can visit while they pull weeds or pick vegetables.

The Briggs place came into view sooner than he thought it would. It was a nice little log house with a garden on the side, and a split rail fence across the front. It even had a gate that stood invitingly open. Minnie sat in the shade of a tree nearby in a handsome pine chair made to her dimensions, short legged and a bit wider than most. He smiled as he made the mental comparison.

As he stopped Big Boy and tied him to the fence, Minnie jumped up and came with her arms extended to give him a big hug. She yelled for Melanie to come outside.

When she did, he knew right away that something was different. She glanced back in the door before coming all the way out to greet him.

"Hello Ben, it is nice of you to visit," said Melanie. "We didn't know you were in the settlement. Isn't it nice that Reverend Brown has come to stay now? The people here can have a real church and everything. Ben you remember Reverend Brown don't you?"

The preacher stepped out of the door and stood beside Melanie. He slid his arm around the back of her waist. Ben was shocked. It was obvious that they had been courting.

"Melanie, what is this? Are you seeing him?"

"Well Ben, a girl does get lonesome," she replied. She had deliberately increased her southern accent until it was a heavy drawl.

"You haven't done anything to advance our relationship. This is the first I have seen you since the building of Jed's house. Why it has been forever and all you have been doing is staying with those horses and in that dirt house of yours."

"Melanie, I thought you were going to marry me! You said you would as soon as you could leave your folks. You said we would be married this fall!"

"I'm sorry Ben, but that is just foolish talk. You must have misunderstood. Why, we hardly know each other. I hope we can still be friends."

Ben swung up on Big Boy and kicked him into his fastest gallop heading farther out of town. He had intended to go back after his visit with her and spend time with Tom and Gentle Fawn and with Sam and Helen. Now all he wanted to do was get back to the hut and never see that settlement again!

He felt a cold numbness inside, as if his chest would explode. He couldn't stuff one more bad feeling inside. He was hurt and angry. How could she betray him that way? He didn't realize it but he was clenching his jaws until the discomfort made him stop, and at that moment he knew that his thoughts had kept him from using good judgment. Big Boy's head was hanging down. He had continued at the fast pace so long that even the strongest of horses was spent.

When Ben stopped Big Boy's sides were heaving. Ben knew that in his pain he had unintentionally mistreated his big friend.

"Oh Big Boy, I am so sorry!" He felt terrible. He pulled the saddle off and the bedroll. He removed the bridle and the horse stood beside him totally unfettered.

"Go ahead, you can run away! I deserve it! Look at you. How could you run away? You are too tired! I should be whipped. I promised you I would never mistreat you and then I do this. Why should Melanie want me? Why should anyone?"

He rambled on as he led Big Boy to the edge of the river for a cool drink. Ben gathered dry grass and rubbed the sweating horse, dipping it into the river and smoothing his coat until a natural breathing rhythm had returned.

"You poor boy, you don't deserve to be treated like this. Forgive me Big Boy, Oh, God forgive me." Ben began to cry. Tears slid down his face and silent sobs caught in his throat. He continued to rub the horse, not really seeing what he was doing. He had bottled his emotions for so long that he wasn't sure which pain had opened the floodgates, but now, here, where he was totally alone, he allowed the release to come. He rested his forehead on his horse's neck and stood there feeling the pain and the disappointment that Melanie had caused. He mourned the loss of his friend, Slim, and experienced the fear and pain again of almost loosing

Beth. Then he thought of Bold One and the tiny baby that rested in the ground near her. It had all built up inside and now he was starting to deal with it all, in his own time.

Big Boy laid his head over Ben's shoulder as if he were hugging him.

"You are a friend aren't you? I love you, Big Boy. Forgive me for breaking my promise to you. It will never happen again." He put his arms around the horse's neck and scratched his ears and led him where a stand of sweet grass was growing and made camp for the night.

Ben opened his eyes to find Big Boy nudging him. The sun was bright in the morning sky. Now that Ben had been able to release what he had been holding inside, he had slept long and soundly. Big Boy was eager to get underway.

After selecting a big piece of dried meat and taking an inventory of his saddle bags he realized that he wanted to go back to the settlement to see his friends and to see if he could get a first reader book for Joshua. He still had the carved knives and he knew that Sam would issue credit until all the fall goods were brought into the trading post. The trip back past the Brigg's place was uncomfortable, but he looked straight ahead and pictured Joshua's face when he received the book. Sam and Tom were sitting in chairs in front of the store when he rode up. They greeted him with hugs and handshakes and said they had heard that he had come and were glad that he had finally come to see them.

Ben sat down on the new board sidewalk and leaned against a post that supported the porch roof. The men settled back in their chairs and listened as he told them of the events of the months since they had helped with the building of Jed and Beth's house.

Rose walked to the store and was happy and surprised to see Ben. He jumped up and gave her a little hug. He explained that he couldn't leave town without seeing her and getting her advice on a first reader for Joshua.

"Ben, I need to go in the store for just a minute and then if you will follow me back to my house, I have just the perfect book for him. You might want to buy a slate and chalk while you are here so that he can practice his letters and numbers."

"Thanks, Rose, that is a good idea. I didn't even think of that," admitted Ben "Joshua and Mary, his mother, and Adam are staying with us now. Slim is gone. He was killed in an Indian raid."

"Yes! I was so sorry to hear that. Well I hope and pray they are all doing well. They are nice people," said Rose. "I remember Mary. We had a nice talk while we were working on the quilt. If there is anything I can do for that poor woman you let me know."

"Thanks Rose." She entered the store shaking her head and frowning. He hadn't gone into the whole story.

Ben followed her into the store to look around. He decided that he would take cloth and thread. He put the slate and tin of chalk on the counter and told Helen he would be back, as he followed Rose out of the little store.

Rose insisted that he stay long enough to eat a light lunch that included a piece of pie she had baked that morning. He left with two books and she refused to take a thing for them. He would have gladly given one of the carved bone knives to her in trade.

At the store he found that his selected items were on the top of a growing pile. Sam and Helen were generous people. They had added sugar and coffee, a hair comb, two dress lengths of material and spools of thread, a small metal mirror and a spool of ribbon to match the pieces of cloth.

"Hey hold on, I can't afford all this stuff!"

"You don't have to. Please take it to help out. Let Beth choose the one she likes and give Mrs. Parker the other piece."

"That's very kind of you both. I did bring these to use to trade," offered Ben as he placed the knives on the counter.

"Ben these are beautiful!" said Sam. "You always bring something fine and unusual. They are more than enough." Helen had put her boys down for a nap, so Ben just peeked at them quietly.

"It makes things a lot easier living in the back of the store now," said Helen. We still have some things to finish but it's getting better all the time.

"I try to work on it when we have a slow time." explained Sam.

Ben walked over to see Tom and to say hello to Gentle Fawn and the twins. He was shocked at the size of the children. Both of the twins were talking now. Stormy was a little taller than his sister, Anne, but both were brown from the sun and smiled easily. He hugged Gentle Fawn.

"My wedding is off, so I won't be coming back in September," he explained, "but I know that Beth, Jed and Johnny will make it this fall, to do some trading and to get winter supplies." She offered him a meal but he explained that he had just eaten with Rose.

Ben stopped at the blacksmith shop to see Matthew Morgan.

"Hi Matt, how are you doing?"

"Great, Ben. It is good to see you again." He said as they shook hands and slapped each other on the back. "Hi there Big Boy," Matt said as he patted the rump of the big horse. "It looks like you are getting along well with this big guy."

"We have come to an agreement. He doesn't bite me and I don't bite him," said Ben laughing. "I need to have you check his shoes, Matt.

Matt lifted a hind foot placing it between his knees as he dug out a stone. "They need to be changed, Ben. This one is worn down thin and it's loose. As heavy as he is, he could hurt his hooves if they aren't taken care of. You don't want him to pull up lame."

"Matt, I won't be able to pay you until one of us comes back, and that will be fall."

"I would be glad to take a half-bushel of potatoes or some seed corn when it is ready, whatever you bring will be fine."

"It's a deal. They chatted between hammer blows on glowing hot shoes until the job was done.

"I almost forgot. I made this new bit with Big Boy in mind. I made it a little bit wider than normal and put this smooth little wheel inside. It will entertain his tongue and maybe he will forget about nibbling on you." They both laughed.

"He doesn't bite me when I get on anymore, but I think he will like this anyway. Thanks for thinking about us."

Ben slipped it in Big Boy's mouth and both men were smiling. They could see that he was feeling the tongue toy, as Ben slipped up in the saddle and headed for home.

He was feeling somehow as if his burdens had been lifted. It was good to talk with his friends. They cared and would pray for him and his family and Mary and her boys, too. He was glad that he had been able to release some of the built up sadness, and that God had led him to turn around and come back.

Tom had told him, that the new footbridges that crossed the fingers of the Silver were built strong enough to hold any horse and rider, even Big Boy. Ben rode him to the first one and started slowly. It creaked and made snapping sounds under their weight, but was stable. The strips of mud between the bridges were planked and fastened firmly. This would save him days of travel time. Big Boy gave a big snort when they cleared the last little section of the bridge. They would be able to travel easily down the path of the Hickory, passed the rapids, around the waterfalls, through the woods, around the bluff with the small cave and passed the Parker place. They would cross in the usual spot by the big oak, cutting two days off their travel time.

He planned to hurry past the burned wagon and cabin, but when his eyes fell on the plow by the tree he decided that he should look around and see if anything else of value could be salvaged for Mary. Her adobe oven sat near the garden. She had done a good job of finishing it. He also noticed that the garden was flourishing without care. This is good land, he thought. He made a mental note that they should come back soon to harvest what they could and in a few weeks to dig the potatoes. The deer hide she had been processing was still staked near the trees, along with two rabbit furs.

He noticed something shining in the ashes of the wagon. It was a gold picture frame. The photo, a round tintype was not destroyed, although the back of the frame was scorched. Ben rubbed the ash off from it and tucked it into his saddlebag. A pitcher and bowl perched on a stump with a towel nearby, and a brush. That little bit of the camp looked as if she had just placed it there to use. It was undisturbed.

Ben decided to use the skid that he and Mary had used when they collected stones and wondered why he and Jed had used skids to get the wood for Mary's bed and the clothes trees, when they had a perfectly good wagon in his barn. He wished that he had it there now.

"Well this will have to do," he said to Big Boy. He wondered how much convincing it would take to get the big horse to pull the thing after he had it loaded. He knew that Slim had kept his harness in the wagon, just in case it would rain. Now he poked in the rubble with a stick to find any metal buckles or rings that he could use to rig a harness for Big Boy.

Getting the rope harness on Big Boy was easy. He had practiced on Ginger many times, but deciding just how to go about conveying to him to pull the heavy plow on to the skid, took several tries.

At first Big Boy didn't seem to understand but then he took a couple hesitant steps and "whoosh" the plow slid up and on. Ben used the horse's strength to turn the skid away from the trees and then fastened it to the harness in the normal position. He rolled the pitcher, bowl, brush and towel all in the neglected hides with the rabbit furs used to cushion them. He lashed everything together so it couldn't slip or bounce and chip the pitcher and bowl.

"Let's go Big Boy. Take it slow, Big Boy," he said as he gently pulled on the lead. Big Boy had no trouble sliding the weight at all. His strength made everything seem easy. Ben walked along with him, not wanting to add his weight for the horse to carry.

215

When they reached the crossing, Ben tied the lead to the big oak in the shade and crossed alone. He found Jed just climbing off the bluff. Joshua came running and hugged him tightly. He told Jed that he needed help to get some stuff across. They pushed the large raft under the skid and fastened them together. It was not difficult to float the heavy load to the other side. Big Boy was carrying the bundle from the store, high and dry, on his back.

The women and little ones met them at the hut with hugs and happy smiles. They all had really missed Ben.

"Mary, the new bridges are in place across the Silver. It made a much shorter route and brought me passed your place. I brought what I could find of value for you to use or store as you see fit." He carefully removed the pitcher and bowl from the skid.

"They are still intact. I will put a shelf for you in your bedroom to make it comfortable for you to use them."

"Thank you Ben. They were a gift from my parents just as we were leaving," she said. She tucked the towel and brush inside the pitcher and carried them into the hut and set them safely in the corner of the new bedroom, on the floor.

He waited until she returned, and then he pulled the picture from his saddlebag and handed it to her.

"That is my parents! I'm so glad that it isn't ruined. Look Joshua, it's the picture of your Grandma and Grandpa."

"That's nice Mom," he responded, "but I wish we had one of Dad." She understood, and hugged him before she carried it in and laid it on her bed.

"Me too, Joshua, me too," she said softly. Ben lifted down the bundle of things from the store but didn't open it.

"I'm saving that for later," he said and took it in the hut and set it on the table.

Big Boy was glad when the plow had been pulled into the back of the barn and he could be unhooked. Ben pulled the saddle and blanket off and released him. He blew a greeting to the other horses as he entered the corral. It was then that Ben noticed how fat Ginger looked.

"Jed did you notice how fat Ginger is getting?"

"She is not fat Ben, she is pregnant."

"I hadn't noticed with everything going on! This is wonderful. Ginger you are going to be a mother pretty soon."

"Should we do anything special, like give her more grain or keep her in the barn or something? I think she is too young."

"Ben, she is three. I think she is just fine where she is. She is doing well so far without us fussing over her. No one chaperones the wild herds and they do what

217

nature intended. She will let us know when she is close and we can move her in then."

"What a great surprise! I can hardly believe it," said Ben.

They continued up the path to the house to eat.

"I am sure that my freshly baked bread brought Ben home quickly, considering that he had been with his lady fair!" Beth remarked teasing. They all laughed and Ben was surprised that he could laugh with them about it.

He explained that the wedding was off. He told them about the new houses in the settlement and the church they were building. Then he simply said,

"Reverend Brown is going to stay there now and he is courting Melanie. They all sympathized and made caring comments until Ben announced that he had a few surprises and that he would be back in a few minutes. He walked down the path near the lake and garden remembering that he wanted to tell Mary that her garden was doing surprisingly well, even though it had lots of weeds.

The lake was busy with ducks. Stump and Rascal chose then to greet Ben by running out from under the pines and jumping on him. They knocked him down into the dust of the path licking his face. He rolled into the grass with them and wrestled and scratched, rubbing tummies and laughing out loud.

"Where have you two boys been? I have been home for more than an hour. It was then that Ben glanced at the den. He was shocked to see that it held a large gray female wolf that he had not seen before and four pups!

"Stump, you didn't tell us you had another family! They are beautiful." The female glared at him, curling her lips to show her teeth and emitting a serious growl.

"Easy Mama, I won't get any closer and I won't hurt those beautiful babies." Ben moved away slowly to the path and then hurried on to get the bundle he had left on his table, but before he picked it up, he took the time to fill both his pockets with jerky.

When he got parallel with the den he tossed several pieces under the pines and gave Stump and Rascal each one. They took it and went to sit a few feet from her.

When he returned to Jed's house, they were still sitting around the table sipping their coffee. Ben said that he had noticed that they had moved the chickens over near the new barn. He could hear them.

"Did you look in the triangle when you were there?"

"No I didn't."

"We left you a young rooster and two of the young hens. Now you have the same start as I had."

"Beth you didn't have to do that, but it's great. Thanks a lot."

"Hey, did any of you know that Stump has a new family in the den? I think I saw four pups!" said Ben.

Jed frowned and looked at Joshua. He immediately thought that a warning was necessary.

"I knew they were there, but I didn't mention it. The mother is a wild wolf, Josh. She may look like a dog, but you must not go near there without one of us with you. She could easily kill you! Beth, you and Mary need to be careful when you go to the garden or that area. She probably thinks it is her territory. Take your gun." he said. Jed was not pleased at all.

Ben made it clear that he was in total agreement with Jed.

"Josh, this is something else that you will need to be grown up about. You haven't broken a promise to me ever. I will show you the wolf den in the morning, but we all need to hear you promise that you will never go near there without a grown up with you." Joshua looked worried.

"Your wolf, Bold One, killed that man. Didn't she?" He paused thoughtfully for a moment, and a sad look crossed his face.

"I promise Uncle Ben, but will that wolf hurt Blaze? She is still a baby?"

"No, not if I can help it," remarked Jed. Ben, I think we better move her to the new barn in the morning. It is farther from the den. I don't want to shoot that wolf, but I would to protect Blaze." Beth nodded in agreement, but she looked so sad that Ben thought it was time to change the subject.

"Mary I almost forgot it with all the talk of the wolf den, your garden is growing fine in spite of the weeds. We need to take a trip down there with the wagon and harvest all we can."

"If you don't think you want to go back there yet, Beth and I will do it," volunteered Jed.

"Thanks Jed. I think it is time that I went there and Joshua, too. It will help us, I think."

"We can all go. It won't take long with all of us working on that garden," offered Beth.

CHAPTER THIRTEEN   BEN AND JOSH
MATURING

"Now, let's see what I have in the bundle," said Ben. He pulled the material out and laid the two pieces in the middle of Beth's table with the matching ribbon coiled up on top of it.

"These are from Helen and Sam. They said you should choose one Beth, and the other one is for Mary." Beth told Mary to pick and she said they were both lovely and that she couldn't possibly. Ben decided to end the silliness by handing the one with the yellow flowers to Beth and the soft blue and green plaid to Mary.

"This is for you also Mary." He placed the metal mirror on top of her fabric.

"Sam sent a ball for Adam; you can give it to him tomorrow." Adam was sound asleep on the big bear rug on the floor. Sunshine was curled up against him.

"I have something very special for you, Joshua. I bought you a slate and some chalk so you can practice your writing and mathematics. I visited Miss Rose, the lady that will be teaching school soon, and she gave me two books to bring to you, so that you can start to learn to read. We will all be happy to help you."

"That's good, and then I can write about Dad on his tree. Thanks Uncle Ben."

"Yes Josh, but I think your mom will agree that everyone should learn to read and write."

"Yes, it is very important," said Mary. Thank you Ben that was a thoughtful thing to do."

"Jed, all I have for us is a new supply of coffee and some sugar, and this." He reached into his shirt pocket and pulled out the papers from Major Connor, making Blaze and Sally legally theirs. Jed read the words that made it official. They had their first thoroughbred.

"Oh, I forgot to tell you. Beth and I have been taking turns giving her mash and she is already eating it and happy. She has been around us since she was born, so she isn't afraid of us like the foals from the wild herd."

"That's great! All is well at the S & J," said Ben.

"Well Mary, I think we better head back to the hut before it is totally dark." He scooped up Adam and laid the boy's head on his shoulder. He picked up his rifle in his other hand and ushered Mary and Joshua ahead of him down the path. Mary affectionately took Joshua's hand as they walked along. Mary was thinking that she was glad to be here with her sons and Ben. If she couldn't have Slim and her own place, she could be content to stay here for a while. She wondered what the future held for her as she fought to keep a tear from escaping onto her cheek.

After he gently put Adam on his bed, he whispered that he wanted to be sure all the horses were fed and happy and that he would be right back. He opened the big door and closed it softly, not wanting to startle any of the animals.

"Hi Big Boy, hello, my pretty Ginger girl," he used their name as he gave each horse some attention, making sure they were all safely in the barn for the night. They all had been fed by Jed and water was always made available. Ben slid his hand slowly on the back of Blaze.

"Sweet Blaze, how are you tonight? You miss your mother, don't you, little girl. You will be fine here. We will all love you and keep you safe."

After giving gentle pats and scratches to Missy, Rusty, and. Buddy, Ben glanced over at Trouble. I am not fond of the name that Mary gave you. You are a nice, gentle mare. She looks to be about the age of Sally, he thought, as he scratched her ears and then reached beside her and closed the window. He closed all the windows and pushed the big doors shut and put the bar on that held them tightly closed.

When Ben and Jed built the barn they had created a slide vent above the windows. High and narrow, it allowed air to come in and a little moon light to filter in yet it was not a size that any threatening animal could use to enter the barn. Before he left he had opened one on each side of the barn to let the day's heat out and the cool evening air to circulate.

Ben spent the next several weeks working with the horses. He worked on riding Buddy until it was a pleasant routine to put the saddle and soft bridle on him and head out across the prairie. Buddy had learned to respond to Ben's directions so easily that the horse was becoming everything his name implied. He had taken

Rusty across the river and found that his enthusiasm for water died when it came in a quantity bigger than the small drinking pond. It was a big challenge just getting him to enter the river and not balk.

Once he had crossed, both he and Missy were getting so they could be ridden comfortably. Sometimes Joshua rode with him on Dixie. They would range in different directions, taking a lunch and getting Joshua a feel for all the land within a day's ride. By the end of summer, Jed had spent quality time on Princess, Surprise and Little Mouse.

Often, Joshua would choose to ride her. He had liked Little Mouse from the first day that he saw her. Beth and Mary took slow rides together in the evening. They had fashioned front harnesses for Johnny and Adam so they could ride in front of their mothers without danger of slipping off. Beth usually rode Princess, but Mary chose between Sally and the horse she had ridden when she escaped the village. She had given her the name Trouble. Not because she was trouble, but because every time she said her name it reminded her of how she had been delivered from trouble by God using the hands of Brave Sparrow and that sweet horse.

All of them had to set aside their other activities when the garden's abundance got to be more than the two women could handle. A huge vegetable cache was dug in each barn and it was filled with potatoes. Another was dug and filled with carrots, cabbage and beets. Many baskets of tomatoes were sliced thin and strung high in the barn to dry. Green peppers, hot chili peppers and bundles of greens added their aroma. At night their plates were filled with the colors of the abundant produce.

Joshua was encouraged to report game along the river. His vigilance made all of them more comfortable, but they didn't allow themselves to become complacent. Beth and Mary practiced their shooting skills and Joshua was taught the rules of safety and how to handle a gun properly. He wasn't allowed to carry a gun yet, but he was learning to shoot and they were all impressed with his natural ability.

Ginger's big baby boy arrived right as the sun dropped behind the trees. They named him Sundown. He was built a lot like Big Boy, and he had inherited her gentle nature. It was obvious from the first day that he would out size his mother in the first year. Joshua had found a second place that he liked to be. When he wasn't on top of the bluff, he was with Sundown.

One day when Ben examined his caches that had held the bear meat and deer, he found the biggest one nearly empty. He knew they had to do some serious hunting to fill the caches before winter. They had lots of buffalo meat left but he wasn't comfortable relying on that.

Ben, Jed, and Joshua set out early. The air was crisp and Joshua was wearing his new leather pants and shirt that Uncle Jed had made for him. He sat on Dixie, trying hard to look taller. Ben had brushed the boy's long brown hair and pulled it back in the style that he and Jed wore. None of them wore shoes. The soles of their feet were as tough as leather from going barefoot all summer. Joshua felt the jackknife, deep in his pants pocket. He had used it for carving many times and had hidden his handmade treasures in a small pocket on the bluff. They were safe from weather and from discovery. He planned to give them as Christmas gifts. He had one more to make. Maybe next year I can make some things to trade in the settlement, he thought.

Each of them mused, lost in their own thoughts as they rode slowly along the trees. They didn't see the bear in the bushes until they were nearly upon her. She growled and stood displaying her impressive height. They were riding with the wind at their backs. Their horses were startled and frightened by her roar. Dixie reared and took off running at top speed. Joshua did a good job of staying on and the boy was able to slow her and then finally stop her. He slid off and held the reins talking to Dixie, as he had seen Ben do with the young horses that he trained. He stroked the horse's neck until she calmed down. Jed rode up.

"Are you and Dixie all right? That was a good piece of riding. I couldn't do better than that myself!"

"Thanks, Uncle Jed. Did you shoot the bear?"

"No she had a pair of spring cubs with her. That is why she charged at us. She was protecting them. Ben said he would rather find a deer or elk."

"Good, I don't much like bear meat," said Joshua, "and it would be sad to kill their mother."

All the horses got a drink from the river farther down and took a while to completely calm down after their experience with the bear.

They headed across the prairie toward the wagon trail; the grass grew tall and golden. The wild grains are ready to be collected, thought Ben. That's another job we need to make time for and the cutting and bundling of dry grass for the lofts. Big Boy stopped abruptly and stomped his front foot. Angel and Dixie shied to the side and backed up. Jed and Ben knew immediately that a predator was in the grass that the horses were able to sense. None of them could see an animal in the tall grass until it was too close for comfort. They stood perfectly still and listened. They could hear rustling and the "hunka, hunka" sounds as the cougar and her half grown cubs swiftly moved along.

Jed was about to say let's head back to the river when he could see the top of a beautiful rack of antlers moving toward them through the sea of blowing grass. He pointed not making a sound. He had to guess at the proper location for his shot. Ben knew that it was unlikely that Jed could kill the elk with his first shot in these conditions. Ben's rifle was ready, too. Jed shot first and the thrashing told Ben that another shot was necessary. He jumped down and ran parting the grass to find himself face to face with the snarling cougar and her big cubs. They had been hunting the elk. Ben backed away very slowly and jumped on Big Boy.

"We won't be eating that elk," he said. "The cougar and her cubs have claimed it. Let's head back along the river."

"Joshua, you are going to have some stories to tell your mother when we get back," said Jed.

"We don't have to go home yet, do we?" asked Joshua.

"No, I guess we still have time to try a little while longer, but let's head back closer to home," replied Ben realizing and glad that the boy had used the word home. Joshua was thoroughly enjoying the adventure. Even having dangerous animals near, didn't frighten him. He felt protected by Ben and Jed.

He grew quiet. It was apparent that Joshua was deep in thought. A little frown rested on his brow. Quietly he asked,

"Uncle Ben, how long will Mom and Adam and me stay with you?" Ben smiled and answered,

"As long as you all want to, Josh."

"Forever?"

"For as long as you want to."

"When I get big enough I want to build a cabin and make the ranch that my dad wanted. Only I want to make my cabin on the clearing in the woods. Then I think Mom and Adam will come there and live."

"Maybe Josh," said Ben. "Time will tell." As he thought about that possibility, a frown wrinkle creased Ben's forehead.

They rode along without talking. Then Jed said that he thought sometime soon he and Beth would be taking the wagon to the settlement to get supplies for the winter. That reminded Ben to mention that he owed the potatoes to Matthew Morgan.

"I will deliver those for you. Joshua if you want to come with us, you could ride in the wagon, or ride Dixie, as long as you have your mother's permission."

"Thanks Uncle Jed, I'll think on it." They didn't see a thing to shoot for the cache the rest of the afternoon.

As soon as the horses were cared for, Joshua ran to tell his mother and Aunt Beth about their adventure, and then he climbed the bluff to the lookout spot.

The next day Ben walked to the garden to see what else needed to be done. The seed corn was ready to be picked and put in the barn. There were still lots of green tomatoes on the vines. The women had carefully left some of each plant to go to seed for the next garden. The shovel leaned against the fence ready for the digging of the next hill of potatoes. He started to shovel and turned the ground, leaving patch after patch of potatoes on top of the ground behind him. Joshua came over to the part of the fence nearest him.

"Uncle Ben. I didn't tell Uncle Jed because I didn't want to scare the women. He is helping them. I saw Indians on the prairie on the other side of the river. There are lots of them, Uncle Ben. It looks like a whole town of them, men, women, and children, too. Some are walking, but most of them are riding on horses. They are pretty far away, but I think they will reach the river upstream by dark. What should we do Uncle Ben?"

Ben grabbed his rifle and yelled.

"Come on!" He hurried to the bluff and climbed the path as fast as he could. The boy was right. The Indians were heading at a slow pace at an angle that would take them up river. I wonder what they are doing here, he thought.

"Where could they be going?" he said out loud. "Let's go down and tell everyone so we can do what needs to be done."

Jed and both women were waiting at the bottom of the bluff. They knew something had been spotted. When Ben told them, Mary's face turned pale. Ben thought she was going to faint. He wrapped his arms around her and told her that it would be all right.

"It is not a raiding party. They have women and children with them. All we need to do is lay low until they get out of the area." He lit the lanterns and covered the fires with sand.

"I think we should put the horses all inside, so they don't call out to the ones the Indians are riding," said Jed. With all of them working at it, it didn't take long to get all the horses in their stalls. The barns had been built big enough so that there was still room for more. The chickens were fed and they had already bedded down for the night. "We don't want the roosters crowing in the morning. Let's quietly put a cover over the pen so that it stays dark until we know they are gone," said Beth. Jed thought that was a good idea. He and Ben placed branches across until they were sure that it would not let the sun through.

Ben decided he wanted to do something to entertain everyone so that they wouldn't be worrying.

"I think it would be fun to all sit around in my barn and make baskets for the extra vegetables and tell stories," he said. "We can hang the lantern high so that it lights a large area inside. We will need some strong ones for the potatoes."

"I think they should be in boxes," said Joshua, "but we can't make those now because we can't hammer the nails."

"Boxes would be better," Jed agreed. "Let's make those as soon as the Indians are gone."

"We need pouches for seeds," said Beth, "and bags for the seed corn."

"All those ideas are good," said Ben. "What should we work on in here tonight?"

"Baskets," said Jed. "We need big strong utility baskets for the carrots; squash, cabbage and beets, and we will need more for the dried vegetables. We can pile the pumpkins in the front of the wagon on hay and the rest of the stuff will keep them from rolling."

"I am going down by the back of the garden and cut a bunch of grape vines for baskets," said Jed.

"Joshua, we could use a mountain of the tall grass, the strong kind at the base of the bluff by the side of the barn," he said as he left.

"Mary, would you gather a couple of big loads of cattail reeds from the edge of the lake? Here you can use my knife," said Ben, "but be careful, I just sharpened it." She took the hunting knife from Ben and felt the blade, nodding in agreement.

Beth knew that left her to care for Johnny and Adam. She carried Johnny, and held Adam's hand as she went to the barn, moving from stall to stall telling the boys the name of each horse and letting them touch them.

"By the time you reach five you will both be riding like the wind," she told them. Joshua dumped his first load of grass and went back out.

Stump went in the barn with Rascal following Joshua. She wished she had a way to keep the dogs from leaving again. She reached for a rope and it was easy to fasten Stump to the end of a stall, but Rascal had figured out quickly that if she got a hold of him that he would suffer the same fate. It was impossible to catch him, but she did the next best thing. She shut the barn door. She sat down with the little boys letting them pet the big dog, which accomplished two things. It kept them entertained and kept Stump from whining or barking. Jed struggled in the door and then after her explanation, he stood near the door to open it while Joshua and Mary

233

brought in their loads. Joshua went out and came back with Sunshine.

Ben soon came in with sandwiches he had made in Beth's kitchen, along with soup she had been cooking. He had bowls and spoons from the hut. He hurried back with two water bags freshly filled. The pan with glue was snuggled into a few live coals to melt.

Jed had gone out and climbed the bluff again returning with the report that he could see tiny dots of light just outside the trees, far up river where it bends.

"They have a few small campfires going and are settled for the night. I couldn't hear a sound from that direction. They are probably pretty tired, if they have been traveling all day. I wonder where they are going and why."

CHAPTER FOURTEEN   A SINGLE RIDER

Ben was right to keep them busy with the baskets. They worked, talked, ate and worked some more. It was late before they slept.

At daybreak, Ben slipped out of the barn and climbed the bluff. He couldn't see anything but prairie, trees, and the river. He quietly took a long walk up river; staying inside the trees, to find nothing. The Indians were gone. The gray smudges of ash from their fires on the dirt were the only things left behind to tell where they had camped.

Joshua woke late. Everyone else was up and doing the usual things. The big doors of the barn stood open and the horses were out. The baskets that they had made the night before were neatly stacked in the corner.

Ben and Jed were in deep conversation that abruptly stopped when the boy got near. They smiled and said they were glad that he had decided to go to the settlement when they were ready. Ben then gave him the job of retrieving the bowls and spoons and dirty pans from the barn. He was asked to clean them all at the lake and put them all neatly back where they belonged.

"If you ask me, we did pretty well!" said Jed. They resumed their conversation.

"Either house would be better than my barn," said Ben. "We need to make an escape route out of the barns, too.

"Well they are gone now Ben and we accomplished a lot. If we see danger on the prairie, I think we should use your house so we can go to the woods undetected. I am going up on top for a look just to make sure it is still all clear," said Ben.

He hurried back down.

"Come on Josh. I will saddle Big Boy. You run and tell the women we are on the trail of a big deer. Tell Jed to come and you can come too, but hurry. He is close!" Ben still hadn't had time to work with Big Boy about being gun shy, but he didn't want to take Ginger while Sundown was still so small. He smiled at the thought of that little fellow. He loved all his horses. I know someday we will start selling some of our herd, but it is sure going to be hard, he thought. Even if I had lots more I would probably want to keep all of them. They get in my heart just like Stump.

Joshua ran back to the corral and put a saddle on Dixie. Jed rode up on Angel.

"All set," he said.

"Me too, but it won't be long before I can use Little Mouse for hunting, too," said Joshua as he swung up.

Ben headed his small hunting party up river and stayed on the same side. Just before the bend, he slid quietly off of Big Boy and tied him firmly to a tree. The other two followed his example.

"The buck was with two younger ones, just behind that pine clump," whispered Ben, as they advanced slowly on foot. Ben signaled that he was going to take the biggest one and Jed should try for one of the others. At the snap of a twig, the deer turned and in a fraction of a second they would have been gone, but both men shot at the same instant realizing that it was nearly an opportunity lost. They hit their marks and were glad they had not hesitated. The third deer was gone before its companions were down. Joshua whooped and danced. He had another story to tell the women. He was so excited he couldn't stand still. Ben laughed at him.

"You won't be so thrilled by the time all this meat is prepared and dried. God has provided enough meat to fill our caches again. I am going back for the wagon. Josh you stay here with Uncle Jed."

It took only a few minutes for him to return. They took the biggest deer first and delivered him to the fire pit by the house, and then he returned for the younger one. They knew that the companionship of the women while they worked made it more pleasant. The meat would be shared no matter where it was processed or stored.

"I'll gather firewood," volunteered Joshua. He had never been allowed to ride Big Boy. Ben still didn't feel that it would be safe, but Josh led him with the wagon to the woods behind the garden and very efficiently brought a big stack of branches unloading it where it would be handy to use.

Jed got the fire going and helped get the process started, before he headed to the lake and walked along pulling the wild onions that grew near it. He washed them and twisted off the dry portion of their green tops. When Beth saw his hands full of onions, she smiled and said,

"Let me guess. Liver and onions! Yuk!"

Mary had started Joshua writing his letters on the small black slate. Sometimes he took it up on the bluff. He still climbed to the top of the bluff often enough to keep everyone feeling comfortable about their safety. There he watched the prairie and the river in both directions. He worked on his carving nearly daily and took joy in seeing a shape develop from a piece of wood. He was working on a relief of the buck with the two younger ones. He had no idea how beautiful it was. He secretly added it to his hidden treasures.

Joshua remembered that Jed had said that he could go with them to the settlement when they went. Suddenly he wanted to go.

I need to ask Mom, he thought as he hurried to find her.

"You may go, but you must stay near Jed and not go off by yourself. Try to be helpful."

"I will Mom, I promise." He ran to tell Jed, that he would be going.

The harvest was more than ample, and the trip to the settlement finally took place.

Jed had wisely taken the saw. He had to cut a few small trees where necessary, so that the wagon could pass through where the horses had gone. The people of the settlement appreciated their trade items. Many of the garden vegetables were purchased before the baskets were carried to the store and the seeds went for top dollar. Big Boy waited by the wagon, resting in the sweet grass that edged both rivers. He and the wagon were secured and the items in the wagon were carried across the bridge to the store.

After visiting with their friends, they returned with all the supplies they needed for winter. Flour, sugar, salt, coffee, lamp oil plus more material for shirts and dresses were wrapped and placed in the wagon.

The most valuable things they bought were a pair of spring calves. They were brown and white with sturdy legs and small bumps on their heads where horns would grow when they were older.

Joshua named the girl calf, Daisy and the boy, Happy. "Guess we will need a few more wives for him, but it's a start.

"That's fantastic. I can taste the butter and cheese already," said Ben enthusiastically.

"We can build a separate lean to for them against the wall of one of the barns. Who sold them to you?"

"A man and his two sons have started a farm on the Hickory, out past the settlement. They have about thirty young milk cows and at least two hundred beef cattle. They brought them all down the Silver when they heard about the Army post. Men do need to eat. I had to coax him to sell me the calves," related Jed. "He was nice enough to sell us two calves with completely different bloodlines so they can be used to start a healthy herd. We went really slow and gave them a ride in the wagon, part of the time."

"Where should we put them for now, until we can get a place for them made?"

"Let's just rope off the corner of the new barn," said Ben. "They are tired from their long trip and will be glad to stay put anyway."

"That should be fine for now," said Jed. "Oh and we bought another sickle and a scythe. I thought with so many animals around here it would help to make the job of gathering the hay for the winter a little easier. We really have an awful lot to do before snow flies!"

Beth and Mary started talking about Gentle Fawn and the twins as they walked into the house. Joshua followed the men and watched as they strung the rope back and forth to confine the calves to the corner of the new barn.

"I think I better go up and make sure we have an all clear," said Joshua.

And so within a few minutes the routine of the ranch returned to normal. The next day Ben and Jed decided to build the small shed for the calves against the side of Jed's barn, nearest the trees where they would have the benefit of the windbreak.

"We could make a corral for them by using the back fence of the horse corral," suggested Jed.

"All that is needed is two more fences. What do you think?"

"With our practiced teamwork at building, we will be able to move the calves to their new quarters before they get bored with their little corner in your barn."

"I sure hope that the wolf and her cubs leave the calves alone. She isn't friendly like Bold One was," said Jed.

"Remember, Bold One was a little pup when I made friends with her. Her mother never did become tame. I doubt if this one will either."

"These pups stay back and won't take the jerky until I go away," said Jed. "I guess it's because we haven't spent as much time with them, as we did with Bold One or her litter mates."   Stump and Rascal followed the men to the house where the women sat in the shade sewing.

The next few days everyone helped to gather the wild grains in baskets, or bags, pouring it into the bins built for that purpose in the two barns. Next they put the sickles and scythes to work. The hay was hand bundled and tied with natural cords then tossed into the wagon. Load after load was stuffed into both lofts, until they were overflowing.

*****

Winter had been a harsh one, with low dipping temperatures and deep snow, but those living at the "S.

and J." had been warm and well fed. God blessed them and they continued to prosper.

Spring came and the prairie turned green. Just before sunset, Joshua climbed the bluff for one more look before dark. It was then that he spotted the single rider in the distance. He thought that it was a young man. He was puzzled by the fact that with the rider he could count four horses. The rider's dark hair and the cut of the clothes were definitely Indian. He wondered if the Indian had stolen someone's horses. He hurried down the path of the bluff to sound the alarm. Beth scooped up Johnny and Mary hurried in the house with Adam. Joshua wanted to go back up on the bluff to watch the rider but Ben insisted that he go in the house. Ben told the women to have their rifles ready and loaded.

"This may be a scout. They may have a raiding party near here." Jed stood inside the front door of his house with his rifle ready.

Ben hurried up the bluff. The rider had entered the trees at the big oak, leaving the rest of the horses on the far side. It was obvious that the oak tree had been used to mark the crossing. He watched as the person neared the hut and looked around, and then headed down the path to the lake and Jed's house.

Ben scurried down the path of the bluff and scrambled through the trees keeping out of sight, to the back of Jed's house. He entered out of breath and waited silently with the others. The rider continued to the new house and stopped, sliding down from the horse, and calling loudly. Jed turned to Beth and asked if she could tell what was being yelled. She shook her head. They waited. Jed opened the front door and stepped out quietly signaling for Ben to stay and guard the house. Ben nodded.

Brave Sparrow whirled around when she heard the sound of the rifle being cocked. The man was a bit taller than she, with brown hair and dark eyes. He wore trousers made of leather. His shirt was tan cotton. He had rolled the sleeves up. He pointed the rifle at her middle as if his intention was to stop her at any cost. He didn't look fierce, but he did look seriously frightening.

"What are you doing here? What do you want? Who are you?" Jed asked. Suddenly Brave Sparrow realized how foolish she had been, entering the camp of the white men without her gun in hand or any means of protection.

"I am Brave Sparrow. I am looking for a woman called Mary Parker. Do you know her?"

"What do you want with her?" he asked.

"I must speak with her." Brave Sparrow responded. "It is a matter of life or death. Is she here?"

"How many have come with you?" asked Jed.

"I came alone. Tell me. Is she here? Do you know where she is? There isn't time for this! I must speak with her now!" The urgency in her voice was unsettling.

Jed wasn't sure what to do. After all that Mary had been through. He thought the last thing she would want to do was to speak to an Indian. Brave Sparrow turned her back to him and yelled as loud as she could.

"Mary Parker, are you here?" Mary heard her then and knew instantly that it was Brave Sparrow. She brushed passed first Beth and then Ben, leaving Adam with Beth inside. She dashed out the front door and ran to the young woman that had saved her.

"Brave Sparrow, what are you doing here?" Mary wrapped her arms around her, starting to cry.

"I have often thought of you, Mary Parker."

"I have prayed for you daily, Brave Sparrow." Jed finally lowered his gun.

"Jed, this is Brave Sparrow. She is the woman I told you about. She helped me escape from the Indian camp."

"It is good to meet you, Brave Sparrow. We are grateful to you. I am sorry about the gun and the poor reception," said Jed. Ben had remained in the house to protect the rest of his family if need be. Now he came out and the others followed. They stood on the grass near the house, still hesitant to get further from the safe cover of the house. Mary wrapped her arm around Brave Sparrow's shoulders and led her toward the waiting group of people.

"Ben, Beth, this is Brave Sparrow. She is the woman that gave me the horse and helped me leave the Indian camp. I will always be grateful to her." They all greeted her then and Joshua came running out the front door. He had been in the tunnel nearly to the woods.

"Brave Sparrow, this is my son, Joshua, and Adam you have seen before," said Mary.

"They are good strong boys. They will be men to be proud of when they are grown," said Brave Sparrow.

"Now that you know who I am, is it all right if I sit down. I have been on the trail since night fall,"

"Oh, forgive us," said Beth. "Come in, please. Sit here and I will bring you some tea," said Beth, motioning toward a chair near the window. Mary sat in the other willow chair, and the men sat nearby on the bearskin. Joshua volunteered to bring her horses and bundles across the river. The horses he put in Jed's corral. Even though they had plenty of grass he added several bundles of hay.

Brave Sparrow could see him through the window, rubbing down the horses with dry grass.

"He is a fine boy," she said as she told her reason for being there, more to the men than to Mary.

"I need someone to stop the wagon trains. You must warn the leaders of the white men that they must not come this way. You see, I have lived with the people since I was young. I have learned their ways. They rely on the animals to survive. The white men kill our hunters. They drive the animals away. They enter the camps of the people. The soldiers kill everyone, even the women and children. Our warriors are brave and strong and they are angry. They have made a strong resolve. They will fight and kill the people on every wagon train that comes this way. They will not let more white men come to the hunting grounds of the people."

Now that her message was delivered, exhaustion began to show. Her hands shook a bit as she accepted the cup of tea from Beth. She feared that she was going to be sick. Joshua came in and reported that he had her bundles just outside. She thanked him.

"Is the old horse all right?" she asked. "He was my father's horse. I have kept him as a friend all these years. Poor Dart Away, he insisted on following me even though he was so tired." Ben let her words soak in for a moment before he realized what meaning they really had for him.

"Did you say that the horse's name is Dart Away?" asked Ben.

"Yes, my father gave him that name, because he was so fast. He won many races when I was a young child." Ben's stomach started to flutter. What was your father's name?" She had a mental image of a tall man that she called Daddy. She had to search deeply into her memory.

It had been many years since that day when she had been grabbed from the wagon and taken by Dark Wolf.

"My father was killed when they raided our wagon, my mother and brother too," she said. "They were Josiah and Mary Slater and my brother's name was Benjamin." Ben's face turned white.

"I am Benjamin Slater!"

246

"Sarah?" She had not heard her name spoken in many years. She couldn't instantly respond. Could this be true? Was this real? Beth and Jed were stunned! Even Joshua understood the deeply emotional meaning of what was happening.

"I am Sarah!" She said. She started to stand and collapsed to the floor. Her legs wouldn't hold her. Ben scooped her up and cradled her in his arms as if she were the small child that he had lost. His tears wet her face and hair as he held her close.

"Sarah! Oh Sarah! I didn't find you, so God sent you to me! Thank you God! Oh thank you." Beth and Mary were both crying. Even Jed and Joshua had tears in their eyes.

CHAPTER FIFTEEN   SARAH

Sarah woke to find herself in a bed with sheets and a yellow wool blanket. She looked around the room to see the sunshine streaming in the open window. She could hear the birds in the trees beyond the house and Adam was jabbering to his mother in the next room. Beth and Mary were laughing at his comment.

"No Adam, you can't ride the white horsey. It belongs to Sarah."

"Sarah looked at herself as she swung her feet out of bed. She was wearing a long white gown. Her skin felt clean. She could remember someone had helped her bathe and change clothes. Her braids were out and her hair had been brushed. It hung long and loosely. She couldn't clearly remember any of it. She wondered how long she had slept.

Beth heard the rustle of the bed as Sarah got out.

"Sarah, the men are gone. You can come out in your night gown," said Mary. Sarah stepped into the main room and for the first time, began to see the cozy room.

When her bare feet touched the bear rug she looked down to see Adam playing with a wooden horse.

"Hello, young man. I see that you like horses." He nodded shyly and then mustered the courage to say,

"Adam rides the white horsey?"

"Well, we will have to see about that, won't we?" Mary held her hand out toward Sarah, and asked her to sit with them at the table. Beth poured her a cup of tea and gave her a thick slice of fresh bread with wild raspberry jam.

"Sarah, you were so tired when you arrived. I don't know how much you remember of yesterday. I am Beth. I am Jed's wife. We are all glad that you are back with your family. Sarah, you are welcome here."

"Thank you Beth and thank you, Jesus, for bringing me to a home filled with warmth and love." She bit the bread and sipped the tea. Before long she was eating eggs and fried potatoes. She had not eaten a good meal for several days. They had offered her food but all she had taken was sips of tea.

"Jed and Ben have gone to Fort Connor. Major Benet will send a unit to warn and protect the wagon trains. Sarah, they will not stop coming. They will simply carry more arms and be more on guard. There will be war and there is nothing that any of us can do to stop it," said Beth sadly.

Later, as Sarah pulled her clothes on, she discovered that they had been scrubbed and were clean, soft and dry. She walked out to see her horses. She was surprised at how well Dart Away looked.

"He likes the barn," said Joshua, "We didn't even have to tell him. He went in by himself last night."

"Perhaps he remembered being in a barn when he was younger," she said.

"I like the white horse. What is his name?" asked Joshua.

"He is Moon Boy and his mother is Pretty Mother. The brown one doesn't really have a name. He is a hunting pony that many people can use."

"He should have a name. Let's call him Brownie, if that's alright with you. I think horses like to have a name just like people do."

"I think you are right and that is a good name."

Sarah had been there more than a week. She had finally built up the courage to take the color remover to the river and with great resolve, she used it to scrub every bit of the dye from her naturally pale blond hair. The fumes had been so bad that it had made her ill. She was grateful that the river also carried that away as she continued to scrub and rinse. Her hands and scalp were tender from the harsh ammonia. Beth had given her soap to use to try to remove the smell, once the color of the nut casing dye was gone. Sarah could feel the awful tangled mess that once was long, strong hair. She poured the rendered bear fat onto her hair and gently began to smooth it down with her fingers. Bit by bit the hair relaxed and hung in long limp greasy strands. She stood in the flowing water for a few minutes longer, letting the oil soak into the damaged hair.

Then ever so gently she washed it again with the lilac soap. This time the hair hung in soft strands to her waist and beyond. Both Mary and Beth helped her to carefully comb it until every tangle was gone. She pulled it back into a single braid and tied it with a strip of leather.

"You look so different with that dye gone. Now your hair matches your light brows and lashes," said Beth.

"Sarah, do you have any idea how beautiful you are?" asked Mary.

"I have never thought of such things," Sarah answered. "God has kept me well and strong. I pray each dawn that I remain pleasing in His sight and that is all that has been important."

Sarah had worked for days on the dress she was making from the pure white hide. If the people knew that she had Talking Mountain's sacred hide, they would be shocked and angry! She had pulled it from his tent and hidden it when he died, knowing that the people would burn his tent and everything in it. They would be frightened if they knew that she had dared to cut it to make this dress. They feared the spirits and believed that the hide held great power. That was exactly why she had to wear it. She finished the dress and moccasins and tried them on. She practiced parting her hair in the middle and pulled both sections forward letting the nearly white hair tumble down on either side of her face. She held it there with strips of white leather braided in only at the very top. She looked at the folded clothes and knew that she was as ready as she would ever be.

Wearing the clothes she had arrived in, she said good-bye to everyone, saying that she had a duty to the people. She tried to explain to Ben and her newfound family why she had to go back, but now that she was here, Ben didn't want her to leave. He didn't understand and he feared he would lose her again.

"I must tell Chief Dark Wolf that the wagon trains will be heavily guarded. I must convince him not to attack them or many of the people that have cared for me all these years will die. Ben, can't you see? Please try to understand. I am standing in two worlds. One world is the one that you know. The other is a world with people that wanted a daughter so badly, they were willing to steal and kill to get her. They have treated me with tender love and respect."

She lifted the rifle from the blanket as she prepared to leave. "Ben I brought this. I'm not sure why. I have kept it all this time. Do you recognize it?"

"Yes," he said as he turned his own rifle over to show her that he had carved a similar rose on his.

"Take it Ben. Keep it here where it will be safe. I won't need it."

Ben looked at her and wondered if he would ever understand.

"I remember it! I remember the day that it was taken. They killed our parents! Sarah, how can you go back there?"

"I must," she said softly. "If it is God's will, I will return. I am leaving Dart Away. Maybe he and Blaze will have a beautiful thoroughbred baby someday. He loves it here. He likes being in the barn at night. Will you keep Moon Boy for me, too? He is very special. He is my most valuable possession. One day I would like to ride on him. Now my sweet brother, I must go." She turned to leave with a heavy sigh.

"Wait, don't leave until we have prayed with you," He said. Everyone joined hands. Each one asked a different blessing for her. Ben's prayer was that she be able to be God's instrument, to open the eyes and ears of the people she returned to, and that through her they would come to know the One True God. She gave each one a quick hug as tears came to her eyes. She felt that Ben did understand at least a little. She swung up on the same brown horse that had brought her. She led Pretty Mother, the beautiful cream colored mare. Moon Boy called to her from the corral when he realized his mother was leaving without him.

Sarah's saddlebags held the treasured white clothes and she carried pieces of white natural chalk as she crossed the Hickory and headed out of the trees onto the prairie.

Ben watched her leave and wondered if there was something he could have done to keep her there.

"Jed, should I follow her?" Ben asked.

"No Ben, it's like she said. She is heading back into another world. You don't belong there. You can't protect her there. Only God can."

Joshua and Ben climbed the bluff and watched her go until she disappeared into the distance.

"Uncle Ben, are you sad?" asked Josh.

253

"Yes Josh. I am afraid that I will never see her again."

"You shouldn't be sad. She is alive, and she loves the Lord. You will see her again. Maybe it will be here or maybe it will be in heaven," the boy said, "But you will see her again."

"Josh sometimes you are so wise." Ben hugged the boy tightly.

"We have animals that would appreciate a little attention. We have all been very busy lately."

Ben and Joshua took the wagon with Big Boy, Angel and Dixie and went to the settlement to the lumber yard. Ben bought enough wood from the mill for floor planking for the entire hut with some left over.

*****

Mary Parker and her sons had spent that first winter with Ben in the hut. Joshua's bad dreams subsided with time, and when he did cry out, Ben would hold him close until he went back to sleep. He understood what it was like to wake in the night and be terrorized by a dream of past events.

Joshua had helped decorate the small Christmas tree in the hut and the bigger tree that stood in front of the window at Jed's house.

When Christmas morning came, Joshua surprised everyone by announcing that he had to go check the look out before they could exchange gifts. He came down from the bluff carefully, with his arms loaded with his treasures. Some were inside his shirt, others in his coat pockets. Each person was awed by the careful and artful work that he gave.

"These are beautiful." Ben praised his skill. Soon you will be making furniture to trade in the settlement."

"I love to sit on the bluff and carve things," said Joshua with a smile. "I like to do the things that you and Uncle Jed do."

After Christmas, Ben and Jed planked the floor of the hut. Together they plastered the inside walls of all the rooms. The fireplace had been finished before cold weather set in. The pieces of Ben's mother's plates and cups were worked into the plaster around the fireplace and gave a beautiful touch of color between the river rocks.

CHAPTER SIXTEEN   EVENTFUL TRIP

That same spring Mary and Ben planned a trip to the settlement. She was skilled with a needle and during the winter she had made men's shirts to trade at the store. Ben had spent evenings carving and teaching Josh. They had made and carved headboards for full size beds. The side rails and footboards were plain, but the intricate designs and pictures on the headboards were decoration enough. They loaded the wagon carefully wrapping the wood and separating the pieces with hay to prevent any scratches. Jed had made wooden cups and bowls. The store was always glad to have them. Many people came in looking for dishes, to replace plates, cups and bowls broken along the trail.

Ben stopped the wagon on Mary's property. Joshua and Adam disappeared into the woods to find the spring. "Mary if you had a choice, if the cabin was rebuilt, would you rather live here?" She didn't know how to answer. Her mind was in a spin. He wants me to move out, she thought. Why shouldn't he? I just happened into his life and home. Just because I have grown to love him, doesn't mean that he loves me back. He is younger than I am. He has been taking care of us ever since that horrible day when Slim was killed. How could I be so stupid? I should have found a place of my own in the settlement. There is probably a job for me there.

Ben was puzzled by her silence. He had wanted to hear her say that she was happy with him. He loved her and the boys and wanted them with him.

"Mary, are you all right? You look so strange. Do you want to leave?" Leave! That is all he can think of! He wants me to leave as soon as possible. That is probably why he planned this trip, so I would find a place in the settlement. Well if it is at all possible, I will! She thought.

Ben could see by the set of her jaw that Mary looked upset, but he had no idea why. He called the boys and when they were back in their places, he pulled onto the trail through the woods and cautiously maneuvered the wagon through the trees. It was slow going. Finally when he looked at her again, he could see the glint of a tear on her cheek. Of course he thought. She is not angry. She is missing Slim. I should never have stopped there today.

"Mary, I am so sorry. I shouldn't have stopped. It caused you pain. I should have been more thoughtful. I was hoping by now that you could visit there without feeling so sad. Mary I can't stand it when you cry. I don't ever want you to be sad or alone again," said Ben. "I love you, Mary. Will you marry me, now, while we are here in the settlement?"

"You love me? I thought you wanted me to leave. I thought that was why you asked me if I wanted to rebuild the cabin. Oh Ben, I love you too, but what about the boys?"

"What about them? I love them as if they were my own and maybe someday we can add a few more, just to make sure we are not lonely in our old age!" he chuckled.

"Yes, Ben, yes, I will marry you! Ben, what will people say? I am older than you."

"I don't care what people say. It can't be all that important. I never really thought about it." They hugged as the wagon rolled along; and laughed, explaining to the boys what was happening. The boys were happy, too.

"Now we can be a real family!" said Joshua.

"Are you going to be my Daddy?" asked Adam.

"Yup, I'm going to be your Daddy," said Ben.

Reverend Brown married them, the day after they arrived, with Tom and Gentle Fawn as witnesses. The ceremony was quick and simple but blessed by God.

The goods they brought to trade filled their wagon with the usual supplies and a big reel of barbed wire fence. The wire was only enough to start. Ben had decided to fence the outside line of Mary's land. The new bank had loaned them money on Mary's place and Sam's recommendation. Ben had a good reputation. They were able to make a deal for the fence and a small herd of beef cattle.

Mary and Ben talked as they bounced along on the wagon heading home.

"Silverville, I like it. It's a good name," commented Mary.

"Yes, that's a good name they picked for the town. It seems to keep growing. Every time we visit, there are more buildings in town and more houses nearby," said Ben

"I can't wait to get home. We have so much to tell Jed and Beth. They will be upset that we didn't tell them we were getting married."

"How could we? We didn't know," replied Ben.

"Did you know that you have the same name that my mother had? You are the second Mary Slater," he said.   They laughed and then talked about what they would like to eventually do.

"We could build a real house someday." Ben said enthusiastically.

"We have a wonderful house already! It is cool in summer and warm in the winter," said Mary.

"Ben you know by now that I am not a person that needs a new house to be happy. Proverbs 13-7 NIV says "One person pretends to be rich, yet has nothing; another pretends to be poor, yet has great wealth." We have everything we need and more. As far as I am concerned we are very rich, Ben."

"Yes, God is good. He has taken care of us and given to us from His great bounty." He reached over and pulled her close on the seat as the wagon rolled slowly through the trees.

"We probably will have to add on in time, don't you think?" He teased as he kissed her on the cheek and the boys giggled, seeing the kiss.

Jed and Beth were very excited to hear all the news.

"It's about time you two discovered that you are in love with each other," said Jed. "Beth and I have known it for quite a while. Congratulations!"

"We are so happy for you," said Beth. "I am going to bake a cake. Mary, come have tea with me so we can talk."

*****

"What are you planning to do with the range fence Ben?" asked Jed.

"This is to make a small field on your land, for Daisy and Happy" said Ben with a grin, "and we have decided to run beef cattle on Mary's land. We figure that it may as well be earning money. It is just sitting there doing nothing. We have paid for a hundred head of beef cattle that will be coming down from Montana. I need to start that fence right away. Tom is going to be there tomorrow night with the rest of the wire and a load of fence posts for us. He said that he and a bunch of his men would stay long enough to get it strung right. They are going to do a survey so that the fence is right on the line of her 160 acres."

"I should get some fence to mark off the boundaries of my place, too," said Jed. "It would be nice to know just where the lines are. I have been thinking we would need fencing to separate some of the horses. Angel is pregnant again and I think it is from Big Boy but Buddy was cozying up to her before they were separated. Guess we will be able to tell when the foal arrives, but that's why we need to have the choice of who we put with the mares."

"It would be better if we put the girls exclusively with the one we want. Big Boy thinks they are all his, but I am not sure that is such a good idea," agreed Ben.

"It isn't for him to decide, but he sure will add strength and stamina to the bloodline on this ranch for the horses that we breed for the army. That's why we need to make separate fields, so we are in control and can be selective. There is a lot more work we should do. Our base stock is really important. It is the foundation for generations of horses to come. I must say that I think the barbed wire is too harsh to use for our horses. I would like to see box fence installed and high enough to keep our jumpers in and that wild stallion out."

"Jed it is exciting isn't it? Just think of this ranch in ten years! But right now we need to cut hay and stack it on Mary's land so that we have it if the winter becomes uncommonly hard. I don't want to lose even one of the cattle. They will bring in money so we can keep growing our horse herds," said Ben

"I hope we will have time to get everything done," said Jed.

After Tom and his crew finished the fence and the gates were in place, they all took a picnic down and created a mountain with bundles of dry grass, inside the edge of the woods where it would be somewhat protected by the dense trees. They cut branches and tied them across the top to further protect the bundles from the weather.

"This is such rich pasture that it shouldn't be needed but if we run into a really bad stretch of winter, at least we will be ready," Ben said. "You had a good idea when you suggested that we cut grass from the open prairie and roll it into the gates. That gave us extra grass without using what is naturally there inside the fence."

"This is a good thing Ben. We are building something new and wonderful for the boys on the ashes of a sad past. I think maybe Joshua will rebuild the cabin on the hill someday for his wife. That would be nice," said Mary.

"Maybe we should get a small one built for him. The law says we have to build on the land within five years. We could put it on the hill or build it in the woods on the clearing. I got the impression that he rather likes that spot. When we were hunting he said that he would like to build there someday."

"That is interesting. As busy as we keep him, it surprises me that he would be thinking of that." Mary was smiling as she said it.

Tom's men piled the posts for the fence at the first corner marker. Ben thought it would be a good idea to put a big gate on both ends of the pasture. The fence ran all the way to within ten yards of the Hickory River's bank and then into the woods including the spring and clearing once used by the Indians. Her land ran into the woods and then the end fence brought them back to the first marker. Mary looked at the straight and strong fence and knew that Slim would have approved. The big trees in the woods will offer shelter for the cattle. Maybe we can make some kind of additional shelter as time allows, she thought. The cattle were being brought the long way down the Silver and along the wagon trail and then across the prairie.

Two weeks after the fence was finished the cattle arrived. Mary said she thought they looked quite frightening. She was glad she didn't have to do anything with them.

"I don't like their big horns," she said.

"You should see the cattle coming up from Texas!" said Ben. "A man at the store told me that their horns make these look short!" Mary shuddered and then commented, "Why would anyone want an animal like that?"

"I suppose they are hardy and survive well in harsh weather and they are big enough to be profitable," said Ben.

"Well, I like the looks of Daisy and Happy a lot better," she said.

"You would make a pet of every animal if you could, Mary."

"Yes, I suppose I would, most of them, but not these." Ben chuckled and shook his head.

They headed back to the hut. Mary rode on Ginger and Sundown was following along beside her. Ben rode Buddy and the boys rode behind, with Adam now using Dixie and riding very well. Joshua rode Little Mouse who no longer seemed to fit her name. With all the love and attention that Joshua and everyone else, lavished on her, she had blossomed into a fine and trustworthy mount. They chatted as they rode slowly along.

"Dad, I wonder who owns the land between our cattle field and Jed and Beth's property. Won't they need to start doing something with it?"

"Yes I suppose they will. I could find out at the land office when we go to Silverville next time. Now that you mention it I saw that the land was marked off, but no name was written on the map. All the pieces we spoke for have our last name printed on them.

"Ben, I know that you and Jed have kept Blaze and Dart Away near each other. It will be fun when she is old enough to see her foal someday," said Mary. "She is fast and her sleek body is beautiful. It is easy to see that she is different from the mustangs. Yesterday, he was standing against the fence that separates them and hanging his head over near her. It looked as if they were talking to each other."

"Her legs are long and beautiful said Ben. Speaking of long legs, did I tell you that Moon Boy jumped out of the corral again and we had to go find him? He is the best jumper I have ever seen," said Ben. Mary patted Ginger's neck as they rode along.

"Ben, I think Moon Boy and Buddy must have a common relative because they are both jumpers and Moon Boy's mother looks like both of them."

"You are probably right. I think of Sarah every time I see him. I hope she comes back soon," said Ben.

"If she does maybe we can build a house for her just beyond the bluff," said Ben.

"Ben, I think it would be a wonderful thing for you and Jed to build a house there before she comes back. It would be a great surprise for her and it would help her to transition, if she had a place of her own."

"Mary, we could even go to the registrar's office and sign for some land in her name so she would have her own place. It could be right on the other side of mine! I can hardly wait to get started!"

"Ben, you should go right away. You could even order windows and lumber to be delivered while you are there."

"Mary, you know that is going to cost a lot of money. How will we pay for it?"

"The Army needs horses, Ben. You told me so yourself. If you fence Sarah's land you could run the mustang herd in there and tame them for the Army." Ben looked at her with a big smile on his face.

"You make it sound so easy, but Jed did say that he wanted to expand the number of horses we have. I will talk it over with him when we get back."

"I wouldn't need to have Tom back to measure her fence line. I watched and I could do it close enough myself, since it's all in the family, it wouldn't matter if I am off a little. I am so excited!" said Ben.

"You are getting yourself into a lot more work Ben. You know you and Jed can only do so much," said Mary.

"Maybe we can get someone from town to stay and help for board, room and a small wage."

"Mary, now you are getting ahead of things. We can't afford to do that, at least not yet."

They rode the rest of the way home each lost in their own imaginings of the house for Sarah, and the day when she would return.

The next morning Ben announced that he was leaving for Silverville alone and he gave specific duties to each of the boys. Mary knew that she would be working extra hard until he returned, caring for the animals and continuing to work on their many projects. She was glad that Ben's attitude was cheerful and optimistic now. He had begun to doubt Sarah's return until they had talked of the plan to build her a house.

After Ben left for town and the animals were all fed and happy, Mary walked with Adam at her side. She had her rifle in her right hand and the shovel to use in the garden in her left. She leaned the shovel against the gate to the garden and continued on to visit with Beth. She found her sitting in a chair on the porch watching Johnny playing with Sunshine and Buttercup.

"That boy wouldn't know what to do if he didn't have those two dogs to play with," said Mary, as she plopped down on the chair beside Beth. Adam ran to join him with Rascal. "It's funny though, isn't it that Buttercup became friendly and stayed with us when the others left?" said Beth.

"Yes, but I think Sunshine, Rascal and Stump all had a lot to do with that. Although I fussed about it at the time, I guess it is a good thing that the men put the big Rocks in the mouth of the little cave so the wolves can't use it for a den any more. It is better that they moved on. I still pray protection over all our animals though," said Beth. "I worry that they might come back. Poor old Stump, he just lays around in the sun these days. He sure has been a good dog."

"Yes he is loved by everyone. It will break our hearts the day he goes. I just came to say that Josh and I will be in the garden this morning if you need us. Joshua went up on the bluff. He promised he would come back down to help pull weeds. Sometimes I forget that Joshua is just a boy. He is such a good help." She looked in the direction of the garden to see Joshua just opening the gate.

"Adam, you should stay here and play with Johnny until I finish in the garden. Beth nodded agreement.

It took a couple of hours to pull the weeds. The garden looked nice. Mary was proud of her son and the clean soil where they had worked.

"Every weed we pull now is many that won't grow when we plant next time," she remarked to Josh as they worked.

"Thank you Son, for all your hard work," said Mary as she joined Beth and the young boys playing together. The day had grown hot and she was glad to be finished. "I think as a special treat we should celebrate tonight. Let's pop some of the popcorn!"

"Yeah," the boys cheered. "If you would like to, you could try to catch some fish from the lake for our supper," she suggested. Ben had built a small safe platform for the boys to sit on. The shallow water near it was not a danger to them as long as they were careful. They had all learned to swim well. After a quick splash to cool off, she gave them lunch. They sat happily on the shaded platform, dangling their lines in the lake and trying to count the many ducks. Beth optimistically placed a large basket beside them, to hold the fish they would catch.

Later, Joshua added water to the corral pond. Rusty hurried over to enjoy his usual stomp. Rusty and Missy had both become good saddle horses.

"Are you ever going to outgrow that, Rusty?" The horse lifted his head acknowledging his name.

Ben had started dividing the horses. He kept Big Boy, Rusty, Buddy, Moon Boy and surprise in the old corral. Jed had helped him make a gate that opened on the far side, to the long strip of trees between the bluff and the river. They had fenced that entire area and the horses could stroll over a long strip of land that went as far as Ben's property in that direction. He had made a new shelter and the fenced land in the opposite direction was for Ginger with Sundown, Dixie, Little Mouse, Trouble, Missy and Sally. It stretched as far as the field where Blaze and Dart Away were kept close to each other but separated by a box fence; they each had a generous area all to themselves next to Jed's barn. She wasn't old enough yet to be in with him. Little Mouse ended up in Ben's new corral with the others because Joshua rode her often. The ranch was growing and soon the simple long roofed shelter would be closed in with walls and a loft, stalls would be built, along with a tack room and grain storage area, shuttered windows and double doors like the other barns. It was exciting to watch the ranch grow.

Ben returned from the settlement with the needed supplies to build Sarah's cabin. Everyone was eager to get started on it the next morning as soon as the necessary chores were done. The men worked side by side putting the little log cabin walls in place, with a big window in the front and a smaller one in the bedroom.

Whenever possible they took time, after the chores of a developing ranch, to work on the little cabin until it was finished. It had a fireplace of stone, for heat and cooking and a porch to sit on, facing the river. They had taken the time to make an inviting bench that sat beneath the window.

The women worked at creating all the things that make a house a home.

The Land's Heritage

Once again Ben had gone to the settlement for needed supplies, and after lunch one day, Mary and Adam were busy in the hut. Joshua went up on top of the bluff. That's when he saw her. He knew it was Sarah! He recognized Pretty Mother and Sarah even at a great distance. He scrambled down to tell his mother.

"Sarah is coming! Sarah is back! She is a long ways out, but I can see Pretty Mother. She is coming! I'm going to tell Uncle Jed and Aunt Beth."

He ran at top speed down the path shouting. By the time Sarah reached the river and started across leading her packhorse, the family was gathered on the bank to greet her. After hugs and a joyous greeting, they all walked to Beth's for lunch. She said she had a big pot of chili brewing.

"What is chili," asked Sarah. "You'll see," said Jed. "This woman of mine is a very good cook."

It seemed an unspoken agreement that they would not tell Sarah about the cabin just yet. They were waiting for Ben to return from Silverville and then, just the right moment.

After lunch Sarah walked with Joshua to the corral.

"Which one do you ride Joshua?"

"I ride Little Mouse and Adam rides Dixie. She was my father's horse. She is getting old now, but she still likes to be ridden. Sometimes we all ride down the river to see the cattle that Mom and Uncle Ben put on my dad's land. There are lots of them and Uncle Ben says that in a few years there will be a lot more!"

"That's impressive, Joshua. Do you help him with all the work?" she asked.

"That many cattle will keep several people busy."

"Yes, but I will do a lot more when I am older. Right now all that the cattle need is right there, grass and water," said Joshua. "I ride down with Uncle Ben when he checks the fences and the water hole by the spring. It's my job to be lookout. I go up on the bluff lots and make sure we have an all clear. I can see for a long way up there."

Just as the sun was setting, they heard the rumble of several wagons. Ben had returned five days after he left. With him came wagons of fence posts, several wagons of fencing and men to help put it all in place. He crossed the river by the big oak telling the men that they should wait there.

He had brought enough fencing for Jed's place. He knew that Jed had his heart set on creating a horse ranch. Once the fence was in place, Jed could start a herd and with selective breeding he could develop a breed all his own.

"Daddy Ben, Daddy Ben," shouted Adam!

"We are all so glad that you are back! We have a surprise for you," said Mary as she hushed Adam and hugged her husband and Adam plastered to his leg. It was then that he saw Sarah coming toward him. He freed himself from Adam's grasp and lifted him above his head, before putting him down.

"Sarah," was all that he could say as he wrapped her in a big hug. Jed and Beth came down the path with Johnny. They had been anxious to see this reunion!

"Sarah, how long have you been here?" Ben asked.

"I arrived yesterday. It has been a long wait!"

"This is a wonderful surprise," he said as he hugged Joshua and ruffled his hair affectionately. He handed him candy sticks from the store, one for each of the children.

"Now I have a surprise for a couple of you. Jed, across the river, waiting for you is all the fencing you will need to do your property line and men to put it in place properly. There is some extra to make separate sections for certain animals," said Ben. Jed was speechless.

"You have it now? It's here right now?"

"Yes, go see it and talk to the men and tell them where you want to start! Jed and Beth, one more thing, I got the property across the river that butts up to yours so now Beth and I can just trade and you will have three hundred and twenty acres that crosses the river, plenty of room to run horses," he said. Beth was happy that Jed could begin to work toward his dream.

"Ben, that is wonderful. Thank you so much," she said.

Ben turned to Sarah and gave her another hug.

272

"Sarah, I have a piece of paper for you. One hundred and sixty acres next to mine is now yours. You just have to make improvements on it to keep it, like build a cabin and dig a well."

"Ben, I don't know how these things work, but how can a piece of land be mine because you have that paper?" said Sarah. "You didn't even know for sure that I would come back."

"I guess I always knew in my heart, said Ben. We have all been praying for your safe return ever since you left. In the morning we can ride over there if you like."

"Maybe I will have the farm that I dreamed of when I was a little girl," she said.

"Sarah", I have one more thing for you." He stepped inside the hut and came back out with the little rag doll in his hand. "Sarah, do you remember this?" She looked at it for a moment in his hand before she reached for it and pressed it close to her heart.

"Yes," she said, "I remember. Our mother made it for me. Thank you, Ben. Thank you, all of you, and thank you, Jesus, for bringing me home." She paused. "Oh Ben, do you think you can tell me all the things that have happened to you since the raid. I want to know everything. I am amazed still, that you are actually here and alive."

"Yes, I will try, and we all want you to tell us, **"The story of Sarah"**.

AN INVITATION

If you do not know Jesus, as your savior but you would like Him to be, please pray the following prayer. Invite Him into your heart. Commit your "New Life" to Jesus. He will be your constant companion, counselor, comforter, and protector. The Holy Bible tells us that He will never leave you or forsake you.

"Dear Jesus, please forgive my sins. Give me grace and strength Lord, so that I will not commit them again. Come into my heart so that I can start a "New Life" with you as my companion. I want to live according to your will and commandments. Bless me Lord and lead me in a life that is pleasing to you. In Jesus' Holy name I pray. Amen"

If you prayed that prayer, you are saved. You are born again. Your soul is whiter than snow. The angels in heaven are rejoicing as they write your name in the Lamb's Book of Life.

Get a Holy Bible and begin to read it. Find a good Bible believing church and start attending, so that you can learn more about Your Heavenly Father. What a wonderful God we have.

I will pray for you. God bless you. Louise Bouck

The New Life Series   Book 3   by Louise Bouck

About the author

Louise Bouck is a follower of Jesus Christ.

Until an early retirement from her fulltime job in 2000, very little time was available to allocate to writing or art. One of the many interests that Louise enjoys is painting on location. The lush greenery of Michigan, her home state and the abundant flowers in her grandparent's greenhouses and flower shop all encouraged her eye to appreciate the colors and beauty of nature.

Later after moving to Arizona, the rugged landscape of the mountains and desert stole her heart and took her artistic soul in a new direction.

Paintings in many media cover the walls of her studio as she has deliberately turned her creative side more to the written word. Hesitantly she withdrew from the art gallery where her work was sold and left the position of resident artist at the local Historical Museum. Louise has written ten books in a series of Christian novels that she is now starting to release for the first time as she works on still another story and another painting.

Books titles in

The New Life Series

More than Survival

Life's Many Journeys

The Land's Heritage

The Story of Sarah

Together

The Blue Stone People

Teewahpanee the Boy, Two Feathers the Man

The People of the Lion

The Lion's Den

Just the Beginning